Henry Oxshott

Hidden in Plain Sight

Henry Oxshott

Hidden in Plain Sight

Simon Fraser

Matador
9 Priory Business Park,
Wistow Road, Kibworth Beauchamp,
Leicestershire. LE8 0RX
Tel: 0116 279 2299
Email: books@troubador.co.uk
Web: www.troubador.co.uk/matador
Twitter: @matadorbooks

ISBN 978 1800462 007

British Library Cataloguing in Publication Data.
A catalogue record for this book is available from the British Library.

Printed and bound in Great Britain by 4edge Limited
Typeset in 11pt Baskerville by Troubador Publishing Ltd, Leicester, UK

Matador is an imprint of Troubador Publishing Ltd

To my wife, Karabeth
and my children
Nina, Aden, Ethan and Eva

Part One

Henry and Finch

Chapter 1

It was 1985 and a cat was in mortal danger. He was not being chased along the street by a large and ferocious dog. Nor was he stuck up a tall tree and unable to get down. He was, in fact, locked in a furious battle with a vacuum cleaner, and the vacuum cleaner was winning. And it had all started one Sunday morning just because Henry had decided to try to clean his flat himself.

The previous evening, his home had given an impression of elegance and sophistication. But that was because in the dim candlelight you couldn't see the dust and the dirt, the holes in the rugs and the curtains, the cracks and damage to the antique furniture, and the vast array of grubby stains on the old wooden floors.

Now, sadly, on that sunny spring morning, it was a very different matter. The sky was a cloudless, azure blue and the low, bright shafts of sunlight shone deep into the basement flat in London where Henry Oxshott lived. It was a good light, and it showed the flat in a very bad light. Dust hovered in the air like fog, and Henry had awoken on the sofa to the grim reality that his abode was a very sorry sight indeed. He groaned. For several months now, he had been without the services of Spit and Polish, the twin hamsters who used to come in to clean for an hour a day. Money was tight and Henry had convinced himself that hamsters were an unnecessary expense. Now he realised that he would just have to do the housework himself.

It all seemed to go quite well at first as he set about 'doing the chores'. Indeed, he chuckled at the idea that Henry Oxshott, a distant cousin of a minor member of the royal family, should be busy dusting and mopping. However, the novelty wore off after about ten minutes when Henry got his foot stuck in the mop bucket and warm, soapy water spilled all over the drawing-room floor.

Undeterred, he decided that he would have another go, this time at vacuuming. Things went no better this time. The vacuum cleaner had a long electric cable which was very handy for moving around the flat, but even more handy for getting twisted around the wheels of the machine or stuck under the door. Then Henry managed to get the cable wrapped tightly around his neck, making it almost impossible for him to breathe. He thought he was going to die. *What a way to go*, he thought to himself; *killed by a vacuum cleaner in the prime of life*. After a long and bad-tempered struggle he eventually managed to free himself and flopped back on the sofa, exhausted.

He really needed a cleaner, but had no money to pay for one. He thought about it quite hard, which was in itself quite hard work for him. This particular cat (who was handsome, even noble, in form and figure) was of low to medium intelligence, and somewhat lazy. But he was a decent fellow nonetheless, polite and considerate, and a cat who always tried to see the best in everyone he met.

Henry came from a wealthy family who had made their fortune a long time ago and then spent it all. So, sadly for him, he now had virtually no money. The flat in a posh square in London in which he now lived had been inherited from his Aunt Dorothea, and the terms of the lease meant he would have to leave it in a few years' time. Furthermore, Henry didn't actually work, and had for some years got by on a small amount of money left to him by his parents, who had both died back in the autumn four years earlier. He was an only cat. Time and money were both running out for Henry. In desperation, he checked his piggy bank. It contained thirteen pounds and sixty-seven pence. He decided that, even though he had very little ready cash, the flat had to be cleaned whatever the financial consequences. Standards, as he often told himself, had to be maintained.

He had kept an old business card that he had discovered when he moved into the flat. The card was from a company providing cleaners and maids. Henry picked up the telephone and dialled the number. There was no reply as it was a Sunday morning, but helpfully the call went through to an answering machine. Henry left a brief message inquiring about the availability of a cleaner, and gave his telephone number. He then returned to the sofa and began to lick his paws thoroughly and clean his whiskers, very pleased with his hard work.

Chapter 2

The next morning the telephone rang. Henry leant across the sofa and picked up the receiver.

"Hello," he said.

"Henry Oxshott?" said a frail, husky voice at the other end that clearly belonged to a very, very old bird, possibly a heron.

"Speaking."

"You rang about a maid?"

"Yes, thank you for calling back. Do let me have a shortlist of the candidates that I might interview. I can generally do Wednesdays and Fridays between 2pm and 4pm."

Of course, Henry could have met any applicant at virtually any time and on virtually any day. He had nothing else to do. But he wanted to pretend that he was very busy and very important, and he certainly didn't wish to appear desperate. Standards, as he often told himself, had to be maintained.

"Well, yes… you see," continued the old bird, "we got your message but sadly we don't have many candidates, you know. It's a very busy time and there are lots of people who require domestic help, you know."

"I see. So how many candidates do you have?"

"Err… well, actually there is only one, but he comes highly recommended and he is available to interview this afternoon."

"He, did you say? A he? My dear lady, you are speaking to Henry Oxshott of Eaton Square, distantly related to a minor member of the royal family. I don't need a 'he', I need a maid!"

There was a pause at the other end of the line, and then the old bird continued. "Well, Mr Oxshott, I don't know if it makes any difference to you, but this particular candidate will work for free, at least to start with."

"Send him round immediately," said Henry as he quickly put down the telephone before the old bird had a chance to change her mind.

No more than an hour later, the front doorbell rang. Henry plodded reluctantly down the hall as he prepared to meet his new helper. He realised that he really missed the hamsters, and didn't like change in his life. *Oh well*, he thought, *let's take a look at the fellow and then I can decide what to do*. He checked his appearance in the large, gilded mirror by the front door, licked his paws and brushed some breadcrumbs from his blue silk polka-dot dressing gown.

Henry opened the door, and there stood before him a stocky, middle-aged British bulldog who looked like he could handle himself well in a fight.

"Finch, sir."

"Excuse me?"

"Finch, sir; the name's Finch, staff sergeant (retired)."

"Ah, in the services, eh?"

"Tank Regiment, sir."

"Splendid! I also joined the army briefly but it didn't really work out after that first morning at the barracks."

"Well, army life isn't for everyone, sir. I have come about the job."

"Yes, yes, do come in," said Henry.

As they made their way down the hall and turned into the large drawing room, Finch took in the surroundings with a careful, steady eye. "Nice flat you have here, sir," he said approvingly. "Though if I may say so, it could do with a bit of a spring clean."

"Yes, Finch, I do agree, which I suppose brings us to your role here."

"What were you expecting, then, sir?"

"Well, not an awful lot. Some light dusting; vacuuming, perhaps; laundry; polishing the furniture; grocery shopping; handyman repairs; breakfast and supper, of course; and perhaps the occasional lunch party. No gardening required, other than the window boxes. I think that's pretty much it. Do you have any relevant experience?"

"I joined the Royal Tank Regiment at eighteen years old and worked my way up the ranks, was promoted to staff sergeant, and for three years I was manservant to the colonel commandant. I was retired from the regiment last month. I have a letter of reference here for you, sir, from the colonel commandant."

Henry waved his paw dismissively. He didn't actually want to read the reference, good or bad. All he wanted at this stage was for someone other than himself to clean his flat, ideally for free. "Well, Finch… how about this? Why don't we do a trial for a day or two and see how we get on? You are welcome to stay here, in the small bedroom at the back of the flat behind the kitchen."

"Very good, sir. Could I make a suggestion?"

"Very well," replied Henry.

"Perhaps you could give me a couple of hours to bring this place up to scratch, all clean and tidy, to give you an idea if you like my work?"

"Splendid idea, Finch. I will pop over to Harrods and do a bit of clothes shopping."

Of course, Henry had absolutely no intention of going to Harrods. He had no money to pay for any new clothes, especially from an expensive department store. Instead he planned to walk down to a café in Pimlico and make a single cup of tea last the whole time he was out. Which is exactly what he did, leaving the bulldog alone in the flat.

Henry returned to the flat later that evening, a little sheepishly – if a cat can be sheepish – as he tried to work out what was a reasonable time to pretend to have been visiting Harrods before taking a taxi home. He had no bags of shopping, of course, and realised he would have to pretend that they had had nothing in his size. As he entered the flat there was a sublime mixture of smells. Henry sniffed the air carefully and detected wood polish, fabric softener and a suggestion of supper being under way, and these aromas all mingled together in a very pleasing fashion.

"Finch, you have been busy. What is that delightful smell, or smells?"

"Well, sir, I took the liberty of polishing the wooden floors, and the laundry was – how shall I say? – a little backed up, so I managed to do about four loads in the washing machine. And I thought it would be nice to get a bit of supper on for you, for when you got back. Seems like rations are running a bit low, but I found some chicken, some dried mushrooms and half a bottle of white wine that was left open, so I have prepared *poulet aux champignons* for you with frozen chips, if that's OK?"

"Finch, you have surpassed all my expectations. This is absolutely splendid. Rations are, as you say, a little low."

"I also wanted to bring to your attention that there is a letter marked 'URGENT' which appears unopened. It looks like it has come from a firm of solicitors; their name is on the back of the envelope. It could be important."

Finch was tough and street-smart. He had very firm views on right and wrong, and he sometimes had to bite his tongue or growl under his breath when people did or said something stupid. He would often show his quiet authority by adopting a piercing stare rather than saying anything. As he handed the envelope to Henry, he gave the cat that piercing stare.

"Oh dear," said Henry, already under the spell of the bulldog's famous look. "I suppose I had better open it."

With some hesitation, he opened the letter, expecting yet another demand for payment from one of his many creditors. Over the years, he had built up a large amount of debts with a variety of suppliers of goods and services including, to name a few, wine merchants, tailors, shirt-makers, bootmakers, luxury grocers, gunsmiths (heaven knows why, as Henry had never fired a shotgun in his life) and, the heftiest debt of all, three different florists. He had for many months spent far too much money, and now he was paying the price. Or rather, he hadn't paid the price, which is why people kept writing to him asking for money.

Henry started to read the letter out loud, expecting it to be yet another demand for an unpaid debt.

To: Henry Oxshott
77 Eaton Square
London
SW1

Dear Mr Oxshott,
In respect of the estate of Sir Bartholomew Butler (deceased)...

"Hang on a minute." Henry sat bolt upright in his chair. "Uncle Bartholomew?" he said, and then immediately fell silent.

"An uncle, sir, deceased?" said Finch (somewhat unnecessarily).

"Yes, Uncle Bartholomew was a great explorer. He disappeared on his most recent trip up the Orinoco River, some years back. He was missing, feared dead, but we all kept up hope, you know. Anyway, where was I?" Henry returned to the letter.

Further to the discovery of the head of the aforementioned individual on the bank of the River Orinoco, and following a positive identification and the issuance of an official death certificate by the relevant authorities, the firm of Jenkinson, Blenkinsop & Blenkinsop, solicitors, has been appointed as executors of the will of Sir Bartholomew.

Although we are bound by confidentiality and not at liberty to disclose the details of his last will and testament in this letter, you are politely requested to attend our offices in Lincoln's Inn Fields on Tuesday 19th March as an interested party.

Yours faithfully,
Jenkinson, Blenkinsop & Blenkinsop

"Tuesday 19th March? That's tomorrow," Finch remarked.

"Is it?"

"Perhaps you should go, sir?"

"Yes, probably, Finch, though the place will likely be teeming with all sorts of strange folk, all claiming to be distant relatives of Uncle B. I know for sure that at least one very unsavoury character will be there."

"Perhaps I should come with you?"

"I think that is a very good idea, and I would appreciate that. But now it's time for bed!"

Henry woke early the next morning. He was not normally a reflective or anxious cat, but even he had to admit that his life had witnessed a couple of major developments in the past twenty-four hours, what with the arrival of Finch and their planned visit to the offices of Jenkinson, Blenkinsop & Blenkinsop.

Maybe, he thought to himself, *Uncle Bartholomew has left me some cash in his will?* Henry had never really had to worry about money – until recently, that is. His parents had had some but tended to live lavishly, and they had never owned a house. Whilst this lack of a permanent home had freed up plenty of cash for expensive cars and luxury holidays, it meant that there had been little left to pass on to Henry. So Aunt Dorothea had, in a manner of speaking, died just at the right time. Her bequest had given Henry a roof over his head for the time being, but there was a distinct lack of ready cash.

Well, thought Henry as he prepared to leave the flat, *Uncle B must have been worth a bit. Explorers are always finding hidden treasure. Who knows, maybe he's left me a gold mine in…* Henry paused. He was pretty sure that the River Orinoco was in South America, but he wasn't quite sure in what country it was to be found. He consulted his *Atlas of the World* and discovered that it flowed through Venezuela and Colombia. *Maybe he's left me a gold mine in Venezuela and/or Colombia?* he mused, as he stroked his whiskers.

"So, Finch," said Henry as they stood on the pavement outside the flat, "we could take a taxi, but it can take forever to find one, so I think the bus is a better option. Well, actually, it's three different buses to get from here to Lincoln's Inn Fields, but that's still quicker than waiting for a taxi…" Henry's voice trailed off as not one, not two, but three taxis all sailed past with their orange light glowing, showing that they were all available for immediate hire. But the two animals took the bus(es) anyway.

The journey to Lincoln's Inn Fields was interminable. Henry maintained a dignified silence on the first two buses, but by the time they commenced the third leg, he felt it might kill some time if he provided Finch with some background on Uncle B and the family tree.

"Uncle Bartholomew was one of five children, including my mother, Eliza, who was the youngest of them all, but she died some four years ago. Their father, Mr Butler, died quite young in a car crash in 1922. The eldest child was Arthur, who also sadly died quite young in World War II. Bartholomew came next, followed by Uncle Crispin and then Aunt Dolly," said Henry, getting well into his stride on the family history. "Aunt Dolly also passed away a few years ago. She left me the place on Eaton Square, which was jolly generous of her. Now there is only one survivor, Uncle Crispin, our black sheep, current whereabouts unknown. He never liked me. I suspect he always thought that when Uncle Bartholomew passed away, I might end up inheriting Yews Hall, the family seat down in Sussex, as Uncle B was always very fond of me and not very fond of Uncle Crispin. I suppose that, now that Uncle B has gone to meet his maker, it is crunch time for Uncle C as far as Yews Hall is concerned."

But the family history stopped there, because at this point the two animals had to get off the bus to make their way to the solicitors' offices.

Chapter 3

The offices of Jenkinson, Blenkinsop & Blenkinsop were just as you might have expected of an old law firm which had been founded in 1823, and had last been painted in 1923. The small sash windows in the dark oak-panelled offices admitted very little light. The meagre hints of sunlight that managed to pierce through the windows illuminated the dust that took its time to float slowly up from the old velvet-upholstered armchairs before falling back down to the floor. Although the room set aside for the reading of the will was quite large, it was also incredibly stuffy from the heat which emanated from six enormous cast-iron radiators. There was so much furniture in the room that it was almost impossible to manoeuvre from one end to another. The floor space that was not occupied by a variety of chairs was populated with side tables and bookcases large and small. In the centre of the room there were also a couple of round tables piled high with law books and papers. Henry and Finch were the first clients to arrive, and were shown into the room by a somewhat twitchy clerk, a rabbit called Mr Hare, which Henry found highly amusing.

"Crikey, it's hot in here. I wonder who else is going to turn up?" said Henry to no one in particular.

"Well, sir, in theory I reckon you could get about thirty people in here, although it'd be a bit hard given the current furniture arrangements and—"

Finch was interrupted as the door crashed open and, pushing Mr Hare rudely aside, Uncle Crispin entered the room. You couldn't miss Uncle Crispin. First of all, he was very long for a cat, and he always wore the most outrageous clothes – the kind not seen since Victorian times. His bright yellow silk waistcoat had a pattern of mice embroidered upon it. His green tweed trousers contrasted 'boldly' with the waistcoat, and also with his long red socks. A purple frock coat and blue silk top hat finished off this dramatic ensemble. He also suffered from a slightly lopsided expression as one eye (which was glass) was much bigger than the other. This meant people always stared at him in a confused way, trying to work out which was the real eye, which only made Crispin more cross. He was greedy, mean and cruel to small animals, though he was possessed of a streak of low cunning. Despite all these bad traits, this colourful cat could never understand why nobody liked him. And the sad fact was that no one, not even good-natured Henry, liked Uncle Crispin.

"Well, well, well, look what the cat dragged in," said Crispin, with no attempt to disguise his animosity. "If it isn't little Henry, inheritor of money and possessions from all of his relatives. Come to scrounge some more from my poor old brother, have you, eh?"

"Well, sir," replied Henry, trying to remain polite, though in the background he heard a surreptitious growl from his canine companion, "it's nice to see you too. Actually, I received a letter from Blenkinsop, Jenkinson & Jenkinson—"

"Jenkinson, Blenkinsop & Blenkinsop, you fool," interrupted Crispin.

"Yes, yes, Blenkinsop, Jenkinson & Blenkinsop," said Henry, getting very flustered now as he tried to keep his temper, "who invited me here today."

"Well, laddie," whispered Uncle Crispin, leaning very close to Henry, "I will make sure you don't get your grasping little hands on my rightful inheritance. I want that painting and it's mine, you hear?"

Henry had no time to reply before an elderly ostrich entered the room and coughed politely. "Good morning. I am Ewart Jenkinson, and I am the executor of the will of Bartholomew Butler."

"Right you are," said Crispin. "I am Crispin Butler, and I am Bartholomew Butler's lawful heir. This is his distant relative Henry Oxshott." He waved a paw limply in the general direction of Henry. "Shall we get started, then?" he asked impatiently.

"We are, I fear, not yet quorate," replied the solicitor.

"What do you mean?" asked Crispin angrily. "Bartholomew had no children; nor, for that matter, did Dolly or Arthur, God rest their souls. There are no living relatives other than me... oh, and Hooray Henry here."

"Be that as it may," replied Mr Jenkinson, with an unmistakable air of authority, "there is one other interested party."

"That," said a dulcet voice, "is probably me."

All the occupants of the room turned as one to see a young white British Shorthair cat enter. Henry could not quite believe his eyes, and for once Crispin was lost for words. Even Finch wore an undisguised look of admiration. The animal standing before them could only be described – without hesitation, without question, without a scintilla of doubt – as the most beautiful cat any of them had ever seen.

"Ah, good morning, ma'am; you must be Miss Daphne," said the solicitor solicitously.

"Yes, I am. How do you do?" replied the cat in a voice that didn't disappoint. Suffice to say, nothing was disappointing about Daphne. She exuded intelligence and a profound sense of inner calm. She was, as those who had met her often remarked, a very special cat. "You must be Crispin Butler," she continued, holding out an elegant hand to him as she held his gaze with her aquamarine eyes.

Everyone could see that Crispin was torn – normally he would have exuded a slimy charm in the face of such beauty. But in this context, as he awaited the reading of his brother's will, he feared that her presence could only be a bad thing as far as his inheritance was concerned. So, sadly, greed won out over good manners. "Ha!" he retorted in a manner that carried a significant degree of contempt with it.

"I am Henry Oxshott, how do you do?" said Henry in a voice that wavered ever so slightly.

"A pleasure to meet you, Henry," replied Daphne. "Bartholomew told me so much about you."

"Alright, enough of this idle chit-chat," barked Crispin (if a cat can bark). "Can we get on with the reading of the will? I haven't got all day, you know."

"Yes," replied Mr Jenkinson in a calm and steady voice, "I believe we are indeed ready to begin."

And so they all sat down and the ostrich slowly began to read the will.

Crispin was very impatient and kept interrupting with unhelpful comments such as, "Yes, yes, yes, we know all that", and, "Well, obviously he is dead; that's why you are reading the will", and, "Can't you just get on with it?" However, apart from the odd pause to deliver a stern glance at Crispin, the ostrich just ignored these interruptions and proceeded at his own snail-like pace.

"And now we turn to the bequests," announced Mr Jenkinson after about ten minutes.

"About time too!" exclaimed Crispin, twitching with impatience and flicking his whiskers.

Sadly for him, all this got was another stern glance from Mr Jenkinson before the ostrich continued.

"'To the Distressed Gentle-Cat Society, I leave the sum of ten thousand pounds. To the Society for the Protection of Sussex Dormice, I leave the sum of five thousand pounds. To the Worshipful Company of Secretary Birds, I leave the sum of fifteen thousand pounds.'" There then followed a long list of small gifts of a similar nature to a variety of local animal charities. Finally Mr Jenkinson reached the point in the will that named some of the animals in the room that day. "'To Henry Oxshott, I leave the Holy Bible given to me by my dear mother on my confirmation.'"

On hearing this, Henry licked his paws nervously, more in confusion than disappointment, whilst Crispin sniggered loudly. Daphne, meanwhile, remained silent.

"'To Crispin Butler, my only living brother, I know how fond he was of Yews Hall as a child, and growing up there. I know he loved walking in the fields and on the public rights of way that surrounded the property. With that in mind—'"

"Yes," Crispin interrupted, "I accept the bequest of Yews Hall and all of its contents."

"'With that in mind,'" continued Mr Jenkinson, "'I leave my brother Crispin my favourite walking stick to aid him on those walks in the said fields and on the said public rights of way.'"

"What?" exclaimed Crispin. "What was that again? A walking stick?!"

Henry raised his eyebrows, Daphne remained impassive, and Finch, who had taken an instant dislike to Crispin, displayed a rare wry smile.

"What about the painting… I mean Yews Hall and its contents?" gasped Crispin, tugging nervously at the lapels of his yellow waistcoat.

"'And finally,'" continued Mr Jenkinson, "'I leave Yews Hall, its contents, all the surrounding land and buildings and the entire residue of my estate to Miss Daphne. She has been my beloved friend and companion these last few years and it is my wish that she fulfil her dream there at Yews Hall.' That, lady and gentlemen," announced Mr Jenkinson, "concludes the reading of the last will and testament of Sir Bartholomew Butler, deceased."

Mr Jenkinson then turned to the desk behind him and, with appropriate solemnity, handed the Bible to Henry and placed the walking stick in front of Crispin, who, with his arms folded, was unwilling or unable to accept either the walking stick or the terms of the will itself. He rose abruptly, knocking over his chair, and strode briskly towards the door, empty-handed in more ways than one, only stopping to turn and give them all a very sinister (though lopsided) look. He then departed with the words, "You haven't heard the last of this, you know," before slamming the door behind him.

Silence reigned as the solicitor gathered his papers whilst everyone else gathered their thoughts. What puzzled Henry was that Uncle B had left him a Holy Bible. Why? And as a separate puzzle, what was this painting that Uncle Crispin had mentioned a number of times and seemed so fussed about?

Just then, Henry's thoughts were interrupted by the unmistakable sound of a cat crying. Even when she cried, Daphne did it beautifully. She was incapable of artifice.

"What is wrong?" asked Henry, genuinely concerned.

"I am sorry," said Daphne, drying her eyes as best she could, "I am just so overwhelmed by Bartholomew's generosity, and I feel that Yews Hall rightfully belongs to you, or at least to someone other than me. Crispin seemed so angry, and I fear he is not going to let sleeping dogs lie."

Henry just nodded, a little lost for words.

Having finalised various administrative matters with Mr Jenkinson so that the title deeds and keys for Yews Hall would be delivered to Daphne's hotel in London, the two cats and Finch departed from the offices of Jenkinson, Blenkinsop & Blenkinsop into the relatively fresh air of Lincoln's Inn Fields. They crossed the road and entered the garden square at the centre of the Fields and strolled together in silence without any real purpose, as a steady hum of traffic and snatches of birdsong played out in the background.

Daphne, having finally composed herself, turned to her companions and spoke to them in a soft, low voice. "Thank you again for helping me in there. I am still overwhelmed by events. I am staying at the Cadogan Hotel, but, Henry, could you please let me have your address? I would so much like to get to know you better, and learn about you and your memories of your family and Yews Hall."

Henry gave her his address and then bid her farewell as Finch flagged down a passing taxi and opened the door. Daphne squeezed Henry's hand ever so slightly as she got in the back. Then she was gone.

Henry let out a deep breath and stood stroking his whiskers slowly and with much contemplation. "What a morning, Finch!" he sighed.

"Indeed, sir. Can't say I took much of a liking to your Uncle Crispin, but Miss Daphne strikes me as a remarkable young lady. I wonder what your Uncle Bartholomew meant about her fulfilling her dream at Yews Hall?"

"Yes, Finch, how foolish of me; I should have asked her. And then there is this Bible here. All very odd. Anyway, let's head home; the bus stop is just along here."

Chapter 4

It had been a long, tiring day, especially after the three buses to get home again. So, whilst Finch set about preparing some more food from the depths of the freezer, Henry curled up on the leather sofa in the drawing room, pondering his future. As he waited for his supper, he picked up the Bible and flipped through the pages. Beyond a personal inscription from Henry's grandmother – 'To my loving son, Bartholomew' – there was nothing special about it as far as he could see. It didn't contain a secret compartment. It was not especially old or valuable. When the solicitor had announced the bequest, Henry had idly wondered whether it might be a Gutenberg Bible, one of the famous edition produced hundreds of years ago and now one of the most valuable books in the world. A copy had sold a few years ago for millions of dollars; it had been all over the newspapers. But no, it wasn't a Gutenberg; it was actually a very ordinary-looking Bible with a plain black leather binding, published in 1926 and priced at two shillings (the same as about four pounds in 1985).

With little else to do as he waited for his supper, Henry flicked through the pages, recalling various Bible verses from his schooldays. Then, whilst he was flipping randomly backwards and forwards, he noticed that some words were underlined in red. As he was turning the pages quite fast, he just glimpsed the markings and then they seemed to vanish. Curious, Henry continued to turn the pages, this time very slowly, and after some moments he found the underlined words again. They were in Matthew, Verse 7. "'Seek, and ye shall find; knock, and it shall be opened unto you,'" he read out loud slowly to himself, just as Finch brought in a tray of food.

"Finch. A most curious thing. The Bible that I was given today at the solicitors' – there are some words underlined in it, but only in one passage."

"One passage only?"

"Only one, Finch, yes. I've been backwards and forwards through the whole thing again, and I can only find one," Henry confirmed, before he recited the underlined words out loud. "'Seek, and ye shall find; knock, and it shall be opened unto you.'"

"Could it be a message for you?"

"What do you mean?"

"Well, since you were telling me how fond Sir Bartholomew was of you, sir, I do find the nature and modesty of the bequest to you to be somewhat odd."

Henry stroked his whiskers thoughtfully. "Well, you know, Finch, Uncle B did like puzzles and treasure hunts and all that. He was an explorer, after all. At Christmas, he would always leave a trail of clues around Yews Hall for me to try to find my presents. I was pretty hopeless at treasure hunts, and most years he would have to help me out. I think the only time I succeeded on my own was one year when I found a present in the old postbox at the back gate to Yews Hall. The postbox was there for many years before the postman's route was changed and he had to come around to the front when he started delivering the post by van rather than by bicycle. I always teased Grandma because the wrought-iron sign at the back gate had lost its letter 'W', so I always called the house 'Yes Hall' instead of 'Yews Hall'. Uncle B found that absolutely hilarious, and for a while he only ever called it 'Yes Hall'."

Henry fell silent, lost in deep contemplation, as Finch trotted across the room to take a look at the Bible himself. Finch studied the underlined words for a few moments and then offered the Bible back to his employer, still open at the relevant page.

"Maybe Sir Bartholomew had that memory of your joke in his mind when he underlined those words."

Henry sat upright and stared at the dog, as if waiting for another clue.

"'Seek and ye shall find', sir."

"I'm sorry, Finch, I still don't follow you."

"Well, if you move the space between the words 'ye shall' they become 'Yes Hall'; your nickname for Yews Hall," explained Finch.

Henry sat in silence, but his mind was racing; or at least moving reasonably quickly, somewhere close to a brisk walk. "So," he said after a few moments, "you think Uncle B is trying to tell us that we will find something at Yews Hall? 'Seek and at Yews Hall find'?"

"Yes, I do."

"But why the hidden message?"

"My guess is that Sir Bartholomew wanted you to find something of great value, and he was very concerned that Mr Crispin might also want to lay his hands on it."

"Oh, I don't know, Finch; it all seems a little far-fetched to me. Perhaps Uncle B just wanted me to reflect on life and death, and the Holy Bible is a good place to start, isn't it?"

"Do you believe that?"

"No, not at all. I don't think Uncle B ever set foot in a church after the age of twelve. Probably the last time was at his confirmation when he got this Bible. But anyway, we can't just roll up at Yews Hall unannounced on some half-baked treasure hunt. I assume it's all locked up since Uncle Bartholomew left. And besides, it belongs to Daphne now."

"I don't think she would object to us paying a visit. She seems to be a cat of good character."

"Yes, well, the other problem is that Yews Hall is quite far away in deepest Sussex; and I have to be frank with you, cash is tight. Here I am, surrounded by all Aunt Dolly's stuff. She kept on buying antiques, paintings, and a vast selection of other old, broken bits until her dying day. I mean, look at all these porcelain plates piled up on this table. They are all terribly pretty and all, but I do rather wish that she had left me a large pile of used twenty-pound notes instead!" Henry tugged at his whiskers in frustration before getting up from the sofa and embarking on a long stretch.

Finch stared for some time at the pile of porcelain plates that sat on a rather nice eighteenth-century rosewood side table. He picked the top one up.

"Very nice," he said as he studied the plate carefully.

"Yes, if you like that sort of thing."

"Very nice indeed," said Finch in a somewhat reverential tone as he turned the plate over in his paws. "It's Meissen, sir."

Henry looked quizzically at the bulldog, but said nothing.

Finch continued. "Antique, painted porcelain plate from the Meissen factory in Saxony, Germany. Date about 1730 to 1740, a floral design with rope scrollwork and in excellent condition. Also, showing the correct Meissen mark of blue crossed swords on the base."

"Finch, you continue to exceed my every expectation. What are you now, some sort of old plates expert?"

"My Uncle John – if I'd called him 'Uncle J' I would have got a clip round the ear – my Uncle John, sir, was… well, a sort of antiques dealer."

"What do you mean, 'a sort of antiques dealer'?"

"Well, sir, and I hope you don't think any the worse of me, but my Uncle John acquired most of his stock at night, sir, from other people, without their consent."

Henry gave Finch another quizzical look, with a bit of a smile in it too. He was rather enjoying all this mystery and revelation.

"He was a first-rate burglar, sir, until he was caught. Had a magnificent eye for art and antiques. Eighteenth-century silver was his speciality, but he knew his porcelain and his eighteenth- and nineteenth-century painters too. He taught me a lot, perhaps because he had the idea that I might follow him in the business, but I chose the Army instead. I still grew up to love porcelain. I even spent my first Army pay cheque on a book about porcelain. Anyway, that's how I know it's Meissen. Your Aunt Dolly had a very good eye."

"Is it at all valuable?" asked Henry – very slowly, as he could hardly get the words out. He didn't wish to appear greedy or vulgar, but he sensed there could be some money to be made out of this revelation.

"Well, sir, I am a bit rusty on prices, but it is in excellent condition, as I said, and it is one of their most popular patterns. At auction you could probably get a bit more, but if it was a case of a quick sale to a top dealer in Old Bond Street, I reckon three to five thousand pounds."

"*Three to five thousand pounds?* For an old plate?" Henry was almost shouting the words. "Finch, are you seriously telling me that you think that this plate is worth three to five thousand pounds?"

"Yes, I am."

"Right you are. Tomorrow, I would like you to pop up to Old Bond Street at opening time. You have my standing instruction to sell it and we will split the proceeds three ways."

"I couldn't take the money from you, sir."

"Now look, Finch. You have been open with me about your Uncle J – I can call him that even if you can't. In return, I should be open with you. My parents left me a small legacy, but no property. Aunt D left me this wonderful flat, but it is on a very short lease and I will have to move out in six or seven years. So I am not as wealthy as I might appear. In the interest of full disclosure, I was not at Harrods when I left the flat the other day whilst you were tidying up. I was actually hiding in a café in Pimlico, trying to make one cup of tea last a very long time."

"I know, sir."

"What?"

"I called Harrods to ask you what time you might like your supper. They explained that they were very disappointed that you were not at the shop in person, as they were very keen to speak to you about some rather large unpaid bills."

"You didn't give them my address, did you, Finch?"

"No, I pretended to have a coughing fit and rang off immediately."

"Good. Anyway, you identified this plate, not me, so you deserve a fair share. I am really not sure when I am going to be able to pay you anything else, but I am rapidly finding you indispensable, Finch."

"You mentioned splitting the money three ways, sir. If a third is going to go to me and another third to you, who does the final third belong to?"

"Jack Barclay," replied Henry.

There was a moment's pause as Finch thought this through. "Jack Barclay, the Rolls-Royce dealer?"

"Yes, indeed. There is an outstanding bill of just shy of a thousand pounds for the storage and recent service of a motor vehicle, which I need to pay as a matter of some urgency. After you suggested that I open the letter from the solicitors the other night, I must confess that I had a pang of conscience and opened a few other letters too. That was the most pressing. But on the bright side, Finch, it does give us a means of transportation to Yews Hall. We can now roll up in the Roller. I assume that you can drive, given that you were in the Tank Regiment?"

Finch ignored the question, but spoke quietly. "That was the car that my Uncle John always dreamed of buying. He even tried to steal a few of them. He would be so amused to think that one day his nephew might be invited to drive one."

"It was Aunt Dolly's. She used to drive it around the West of England on her many antique trips. She always claimed it was the big boot that made her buy one. The problem was that she always had to park a mile away from all the antique dealers so that they didn't think she had too much money!"

"With your permission, sir, if I can sell the plate on Old Bond Street, I will pick up the car myself from Jack Barclay on Berkeley Square. It's just around the corner. Perhaps you can call them and explain that a trusted member of your staff will pick it up late tomorrow morning."

Henry nodded his approval. He really liked the idea that he now had a trusted member of staff.

Chapter 5

The following morning, Henry paced the room anxiously from the moment Finch left on his mission to sell the Meissen plate. He tugged nervously at his whiskers. What if Finch was wrong? What if the plate was only worth a few pounds? Or – even worse – what if it was a worthless fake? Henry had already become so fixated on the idea that he would, for the first time in years, get to enjoy Aunt Dolly's Rolls-Royce that he couldn't focus on anything else.

At around 11.30, the telephone rang. Henry picked it up, expecting the worst. Perhaps it was Finch reporting on an unsuccessful trip to Old Bond Street? But the news that came down the telephone line was worse – much worse.

"Is that Henry Oxshott?" The voice was unmistakable.

"Daphne!" Henry replied. It wasn't a question, more of an affirmation.

"Henry, something terrible has happened. Yews Hall has been burgled. It's been ransacked."

"What?" Henry replied in disbelief.

"It happened last night, or at least sometime in the last day or two. The police say they were contacted this morning by the housekeeper who still goes into the house once a week. They managed to get hold of me via the solicitor. Apparently, Bartholomew left the housekeeper a tidy sum in advance so she would continue to look after Yews Hall even when he was abroad for a long time and didn't know when he would be back. The curious thing is that, according to her, nothing seems to be missing. I'm afraid to go down there on my own. Do you think you could come with me?"

Henry swelled with pride. "Of course, I'd be delighted to accompany you. We can take my car. It does seem odd that nothing was taken. As a matter of fact, I was going to ask you anyway if I could pay a visit to Yews Hall as something has come up relating to Uncle B's will."

"Oh really?" replied Daphne, sounding nervous at the mention of the will, but not as nervous as Henry, who realised that he had offered to drive Daphne down to Yews Hall, but wasn't yet sure whether he would actually have a car.

"I can explain on the way down to Sussex," he said. "Look, can I call you back in an hour or so? Finch is… err… running some errands."

"Yes, of course. Please do bring Finch too; I would feel much safer if he came along with us."

Henry felt a sharp pang of disappointment. He had thought, with some pride, that the role of Daphne's protector would fall to him. But pride, as they say, goes before a fall. "Yes of course, I'll call you back shortly," he said with a touch of despondency, as he was now feeling a bit deflated and even more anxious about the sale of the Meissen plate.

His anxiety was short-lived. He heard a familiar car horn honk outside the flat, opened the shutters at the window and beheld a marvellous sight. For there was Finch standing ramrod-straight, with a huge grin on his face. It was the first time Henry had seen any bulldog grin in that way, let alone his companion, who often had a solemn demeanour. But then he realised the cause of Finch's happiness. For parked at the kerbside was a gleaming and immaculate 1979 Rolls-Royce Silver Shadow saloon finished, as the original particulars of sale had stated, in nutmeg-brown paint with an interior of beige Connolly hide.

Henry waved back through the window and raced round to open the front door. He called up, "So did it all go smoothly then, Finch?"

"Yes, indeed," replied the bulldog as he trotted briskly down the steps and into the flat. "I ended up selling the plate to a small dealer in Mount Street. A very small dealer; a mole, in fact, by the name of Davis. He gave me what I asked for with no haggling."

"Which, if I may inquire, was how much?" asked Henry, twiddling his whiskers in hope.

"Four thousand pounds. I expect Mr Davis will call one of his clients in the next day or two and sell it to him for something like seven or eight. So everyone is happy." Finch was still in a good mood and pleased with his dealmaking.

"Four thousand pounds," repeated Henry, somewhat slowly, in a tone that was not quite as cheerful as Finch might have anticipated. "Well, that is good news, but there has been a rather dramatic development down at Yews Hall that takes the shine off things a bit. We need to set out for Sussex immediately, and collect Daphne on the way."

Chapter 6

In the kitchen, Henry gave Finch all the background on the break-in at Yews Hall, and watched as the bulldog prepared some food and drink for the journey down to Sussex, before the two of them set off in the Rolls-Royce for Daphne's hotel.

Henry was excited. Although he was very concerned about the break-in, he was looking forward to the journey down to the house. He saw himself sitting with Daphne in the back of the Shadow, with Finch at the wheel. At first it would be slow progress as they made their way out of London, through Brixton and Dulwich and then the meandering suburbs of Bromley and Biggin Hill, but once in Kent they would commence the swifter route through country roads that would take them all the way to their ultimate destination. Henry imagined chatting amiably with Daphne the entire journey, intriguing her with tales of Yews Hall and his extended family.

Of course, it didn't quite work out like that. She had arranged for the porter to deposit "a few pieces of luggage" on the pavement outside the hotel, and it took some time to load it all into the boot of the car. In fact, there were so many boxes, bags and suitcases that Henry lost count after ten. In an effort to look gallant, he tried to help the porter load the luggage into the boot, and in doing so managed to bang his shin on the back bumper, hit his head on the raised boot hatch, and drop an especially heavy valise on his toes. So he was extremely hot and bothered and in some pain at the very point at which Daphne announced that she always got awfully carsick and would prefer to sit in the front. Henry was about to announce, with some frustration, that he had never, ever heard of anyone being carsick in a Rolls-Royce, but decided to bite his tongue. He then *actually* bit his tongue, which was a cause of further pain and discomfort.

There then followed a brief discussion about who should drive, as of course Henry now wanted to sit in the front with Daphne. But Finch refused point-blank to be "chauffeured rather than chauffeur". Henry therefore, somewhat reluctantly, ended up alone in the back of the car. It reminded him of his days as an only child. What made matters worse was that Daphne and Finch seemed to get on like a house on fire and chatted away throughout the whole journey, the bulldog answering all the cat's questions about life in the Tank Regiment. Even in the hushed atmosphere of the Rolls-Royce, Henry had some difficulty keeping up with the conversation, so in the end he gave up. Instead, he decided to give himself a bit of a makeover, and licked his paws and legs clean for about twenty minutes. As he did so, he started to think about Yews Hall and his memories of the place. He had only visited once or twice since the death of his parents, so he felt a mixture of anxiety, nostalgia and longing.

Yews Hall had been built in the late seventeenth century, but a huge fire in 1900 had burnt down the original building and the later additions from the eighteenth and nineteenth centuries. So what stood there now was a smaller country house that had been completed in 1905. Although smaller, it still boasted ten bedrooms, three separate staircases, stables and a paddock, a tennis court and, since 1960, a rather lovely swimming pool lined with black marble. Of the four yew trees that had given the original house its name, all had now disappeared. Three had fallen victim to the fire of 1900, and the fourth, as Henry's grandma used to say, "died of a broken heart a few years later at the loss of its three siblings". The house still retained the name of Yews Hall; although, Henry thought to himself, it was now a case of 'seek and yews ye shall not find', and he permitted himself a modest meow at his clever wordplay.

When he was growing up in the 1970s, Yews Hall had been a place of much social activity. Even in old age, his grandparents had continued the tradition of many previous generations of the family by hosting all manner of social events at Yews Hall throughout the year, but especially around Christmas, Easter and the August bank holiday. Fox-hunting parties left from the driveway on frosty mornings in the hunting season, and a large village fete was held in the grounds every Easter. Then of course there was the annual late summer cricket match that pitted Yews Hall against Wadhurst, the local cricket club. It was a tradition that Uncle Crispin would be sole umpire for these matches, and, for reasons that escaped everyone else involved (players and spectators alike), he always insisted on cheating. Why an umpire would cheat when no one else did was a mystery that was never solved.

For Henry, all his memories and impressions of Yews Hall seemed to mingle with each other as they came back to him thick and fast. So, almost as one single memory, he recalled the smell of the freshly mown summer grass at the cricket match, the flicker of candles in the snowy light at Christmas, and the shimmer and rumble of the expensive limousines and sports cars that delivered the vast array of famous guests to the house throughout the year.

Then, by curious coincidence, as Henry was remembering the turn into the long driveway from the main road just after a sharp bend, he was brought back to the present as Daphne asked him whether they were close to Yews Hall yet. This was a time before satellite navigation and smartphones, so Daphne and Finch were relying on a paper road map to find their destination and had got somewhat lost. Henry looked out of the window and was able immediately to pinpoint their position (based on memory, not map) and give Finch clear directions. Not long after, they were turning into that familiar long driveway.

Chapter 7

As the Silver Shadow crunched slowly over the gravel and pulled up to the front door of Yews Hall, the housekeeper emerged from the house. It was clear from her expression that she had been waiting for them somewhat anxiously. Of course, of the three visitors, she only recognised Henry, and she had not seen him for some years now. The housekeeper, who was called Aimee Chèvre, then proceeded to perform a somewhat awkward curtsey (curtseys are especially awkward for goats). Henry did his best to put her at ease as he introduced her first to the new owner of Yews Hall, and then to Finch.

It was only as Henry turned to look at Daphne, lost in awe as she studied the house and the beautiful red and pink camellias planted at the front, that he had a startling realisation. "So you have never been here before, then?" he asked.

"No," she replied, "I only know it from how your uncle described it to me and he really didn't do it justice... it's so beautiful."

"Yes, it is," agreed Henry. "Let me show you around."

So, whilst Madame Chèvre prepared some afternoon tea, Henry conducted Daphne and Finch around the house. He absolutely relished the role of tour guide and, after a room or two, really got into character. You would have thought there were twenty or thirty people on the tour, as he kept repeating phrases like, "If you would all step this way, please" and "If you wouldn't mind all coming just a little bit closer to me, please" as well as "Yews Hall holds many secrets, none of which it shall ever divulge." But it made Daphne laugh (which pleased him immensely), and he also shared some lovely stories about his own childhood memories of the house, and showed them some of his favourite views over the gardens from various upstairs windows. If his aim had been to impress Daphne and Finch with the glories of Yews Hall, he didn't really need to try that hard. His two guests were already captivated by it.

The house enjoyed a prime position in the valley and boasted some wonderful antique furniture and silk wallpapers, as well as watercolours of plants and landscapes from all around the world that were the results of Uncle Bartholomew's travels. But what was really special about the house was that although one could see the elegance and luxury in everything, it had all been done in a way that was not at all stuffy, so it wasn't like you felt you were in a museum. You just thought you were in a beautiful home. On this particular day, as the soft, dappled sunlight cast its spell over the house and gardens, it was simply a magical place to be.

As they sat down to tea in the drawing room, Madame Chèvre provided some more details on the break-in, although all she really added was a lot of French melodrama rather than any new information. After hearing her out, Henry tried to summarise the situation.

"So, Madame Chèvre, thank you for telling us as much as you can about what happened. What we can conclude, from the broken window in the door to the boot room and the fact that the glass had fallen onto the floor inside, is that someone did indeed break into the house. However, having spent considerable time looking in all the rooms, and knowing Yews Hall probably better than anyone else since you have been housekeeper here for nearly twenty years, your conclusion, Madame, is that nothing has been taken?"

"Correct, Monsieur Oxshott. But I also noticed something else very strange."

"Which was what?" asked Henry.

"That the intruder seemed to become more and more angry and upset as he went through the house. He entered by the boot room and is therefore likely to have started out in the West Wing. As he made his way through each room towards the East Wing, the damage and disturbance got worse and worse."

"Good detective work, Madame!" exclaimed Henry.

"So why would a burglar become more and more angry as he went from room to room?" asked Daphne.

"Because, ma'am," interjected Finch, "the intruder was looking for a very specific thing, and all the time he failed to find it, he became more and more frustrated."

"If I may," continued Finch, "Madame Chèvre, are you sure there are no paintings missing?"

"Yes, I am absolutely certain, Monsieur. I have been housekeeper here for many years and I know the house intimately."

"Why do you ask about a painting?" asked Daphne.

"Uncle Crispin mentioned a painting at the reading of the will, didn't he?" remarked Henry.

Finch said nothing. Indeed, for a few moments they all remained silent as they all had the same thought, one they were reluctant to share out loud – could Uncle Crispin have been the intruder?

"Well, Monsieur Henry," said Madame Chèvre, "I should tell you that Monsieur Bartholomew was keen for me to show you something in your room when you next came to visit."

"Don't worry," laughed Henry, "I have to confess, we did linger in my old room for some time as part of my guided tour."

"Well, Monsieur Henry," said Madame Chèvre, "he was very keen for you to see your old school trunk."

"School trunk?" asked Henry in a puzzled tone.

"Yes, the heavy brown metal one," replied the goat, with a rather strange look on her face.

"Madame Chèvre, there must be some mistake; I have never owned a brown school trunk," said the cat.

"I think you are mistaken, Monsieur Henry," she said, again with the same expression. She was talking in a very strange voice too, as if she were reading a script for a play.

Finch could see that his employer was starting to get somewhat irritated, but sensed that there was something important about the trunk, and so he decided to intervene. "I think you should take a look, sir."

"Yes, I think we should," agreed Daphne.

"Well, frankly, I think this is all a bit ridiculous," said Henry, "but with all these strange goings-on, perhaps we should. Let's get to the bottom of it!"

"That is exactly what Monsieur Bartholomew said," replied Madame Chèvre.

"What?" asked Henry.

"'Tell Henry to get to the bottom of it.' That is what he said, Monsieur."

"To the bottom of these strange goings-on?"

"No, Monsieur; to the bottom of the trunk."

Henry rolled his eyes, tugged his whiskers in frustration, and leapt swiftly upstairs to his room. The others followed him.

Chapter 8

In the corner of Henry's bedroom, just as Madame Chèvre had indicated, and previously overlooked on the 'official' guided tour, was a sturdy-looking, brown-painted metal trunk. As Henry and Finch manoeuvred it into the centre of the room, they were taken aback by its weight. Henry made a joke about it, saying that it was so heavy it must contain a dead body, but no one laughed and he instantly regretted saying it.

He then proceeded to open the trunk, and they were all astonished to discover that it contained nothing more than a small bundle of papers at the bottom. Henry let out a cry of joy as he recognised some old letters that Uncle Bartholomew had written to him when he was a kitten at boarding school many years ago. He had been quite lonely at school, and had always relished receiving post from Uncle Bartholomew, who would write in great detail about his recent travels and the goings-on at Yews Hall. Slowly, Henry reopened one of the letters and a tear or two came to his eye as he began to read it to himself. Daphne felt concerned for him as he seemed to be quite upset. So,

noticing a rather pretty postcard amongst all the letters, she decided to break the silence.

"Oh, that's a lovely picture," she said, pointing at the postcard. "Isn't that Venice?"

"I have no idea," said Henry as he picked up the postcard. "Let me see what it says on the back." He turned the postcard over. "Yes, it's printed here: *The Dogana from the Steps of the Hotel Europa.* Hang on, it's got some writing on it; Uncle Bartholomew's handwriting. Shall I read it?"

The audience of cat, dog and goat nodded in unison. Henry proceeded to read the postcard.

My dear nephew Henry,

I hope all is well with you. I had to send you this lovely postcard. I think you will admire this view of Venice, which is

what you see from the steps of the Hotel Europa where I am
currently staying. It is a view that I have come to love, and I
hope you will enjoy it too.
    Love,
    Uncle Bartholomew

"Oh, isn't that lovely?" said Daphne. "He really was such a sweet man beneath that gruff explorer's exterior."

"Well," said Henry very slowly, as he stroked his whiskers, "there is something very fishy here. I have two – no, three – major issues with this postcard."

"What on earth do you mean?" asked Daphne, staring at him.

"First, I have never, ever seen this postcard before in my life," he said emphatically. "Uncle Bartholomew never sent it to me – or if he did, I never received it – so it seems very odd to me that it has made its way into this bundle of letters I do remember receiving from him. Second, Uncle B hated hotels, and I mean he *really* hated hotels. He never stayed in them; he always preferred to spend a night with friends or relatives. He would rather sleep on a park bench than stay in a hotel. And third, Uncle B loathed Venice with a passion. He always regarded it as the worst tourist trap in the whole world, and he vowed to never, ever go there. So I find this whole thing to be very, very odd."

With that, out of sheer frustration and a very uncharacteristic loss of temper, Henry slammed the brown trunk shut. As the lid crashed down, paint flaked off it to reveal a dull gold colour beneath. Daphne let out a yelp of surprise, and Finch bent down slowly and carefully examined it. Madame Chèvre merely smiled.

"Well, that explains the weight," said Finch. "It's not that the trunk is full of anything heavy. It's the trunk itself that is heavy because it is made of gold."

"Gold?" repeated Henry in disbelief.

"Yes, Monsieur Henry," said Madame Chèvre. "Twenty-two-carat gold. Made by a local craftsman from gold that came from the mine at Antioquia in Colombia, to the precise specifications of Monsieur Bartholomew. It is his gift to you."

"So that is what he meant by 'Seek and ye shall find', eh?" said Henry, recovering his good humour and remembering the words from the Holy Bible. "And you were in on it all the time, Madame!" he added with a grin.

The goat merely smiled again.

"What a wonderful gift," exclaimed Daphne. "In those stories of pirates discovering an old chest, it's always full of gold and precious stones. But here it's the chest itself that is the treasure. You know," she continued, "it must be worth an awful lot of money. The current price of gold is about four hundred dollars an ounce. What do you think it weighs, Finch? It must be about fifty pounds."

"Yes," replied the bulldog, "it's about the weight of an army kitbag, so I reckon that's about right."

"So how much is that, then?" asked Henry, who wasn't terribly good at arithmetic.

"It's about three hundred thousand dollars!" exclaimed Daphne.

"How on earth do you know so much about the price of gold?" asked a curious Henry, who was now doubly impressed with Daphne's knowledge of precious metals and her acumen with mental arithmetic.

"Well, you know, one does pick these things up," said Daphne with a wry smile. Her aquamarine eyes twinkled. "But come on!" she said, giving a him a hug. "This is the gift from your uncle, so let's celebrate!"

"Yes," Henry replied, enjoying the hug as much as the gold. "What a wonderful surprise."

He was really quite overwhelmed by the change in his circumstances. Although selling the Meissen plate had brought him some much-needed short-term cash, the solid gold trunk was really something else. Henry was confident that he could pay all his debts and, more importantly for him, employ Finch on a permanent basis, which was why he was somewhat perplexed when he saw the look on the face of his canine companion, who wore a very troubled expression.

"Finch," he said, "you look a little underwhelmed."

"Well, you see," the dog replied slowly, "I am just a bit troubled by the postcard in the light of what you said about never having seen it before and so on. I am sure I have seen the actual painting somewhere before, and recently too. I feel this isn't the end of it. I smell danger, sir."

"Oh, come on," said Henry playfully, "believe me, this is a classic Uncle B treasure hunt, and we found the treasure! I really couldn't have done it without you all. We should all celebrate. Do you plan to stay here, Daphne?"

"No – I had intended to stay but now think I need to go back to London and organise things, to get Yews Hall up and running properly. In the meantime, Madame Chèvre, I would be delighted if you would agree to continue as housekeeper."

"With pleasure, Mademoiselle Daphne," replied the goat with another awkward curtsey.

And with that, they all departed from Henry's room, save Finch. He remained awhile, quietly picking up the postcard and staring at it carefully for some minutes, deep in thought. Then after some hesitation he tucked it in his pocket and went downstairs.

Chapter 9

Once they were ready to leave for London, Henry and Finch went back upstairs to collect the trunk. With some difficulty, they managed to manoeuvre it down the narrow staircase and into the boot room. They then proceeded outside and, after several bumps along the way, positioned it carefully behind the Silver Shadow. Just as Henry was remarking how fortunate it was that the boot on the Rolls-Royce was rather large and the trunk would fit comfortably inside, a loud, whiplike crack shattered the silence that hung in the crisp Sussex country air. Henry was knocked to the floor, and felt a pain in his chest. At first he was convinced that he had been shot, as he saw blood on the brown gravel beneath him. But then he realised that the blood was not his, but Finch's. As another shot rang out and scattered gravel as it hit the ground nearby, he instinctively dragged the injured bulldog behind the car for cover and watched as a third shot hit the very spot on the gravel that was already covered in blood.

"Are you all right?" Henry asked nervously.

Finch opened his eyes. "Yes, sir, don't worry; it's just a flesh wound. What about Daphne?" he asked with some concern.

"Daphne!" shouted Henry. "Stay inside the house; Finch has been shot."

"Listen," shouted Daphne in return, "bring him back into the house. I will provide cover on one, two, three!"

"Beg your pardon?" said Henry, who didn't really have a clue what was going on.

Daphne spoke again, slowly this time. "I will count to three, Henry; then on three, you bring Finch back inside the house."

"OK," said Henry with some hesitation. He was very concerned that Finch, being solid muscle, was a very heavy dog to manhandle (or rather, cathandle), and that next time it might be him who got shot. He also wasn't exactly sure what sort of cover Daphne was intending to provide.

So he was quite surprised, as he dragged the injured bulldog the five metres from the cover of the Rolls-Royce to the door of the house, to see Daphne emerge with a double-barrelled shotgun. She fired both barrels in the direction of a large tree at the top of the driveway. Then there was the sound of a motorcycle starting up, and a glimpse of a long purple tailcoat before it disappeared behind the thick hedge at the end of the drive.

Once inside, Henry managed to get Finch propped up on a chair. Madame Chèvre, who as a young goat many years ago had trained as a nurse in France, inspected the wound, whilst Daphne reloaded the shotgun.

"Thank you, Daphne," said Henry. "Where on earth did you learn to shoot like that?"

"Well, you know, Henry, one picks these things up," said Daphne with a smile.

"That's the second time you've said that," muttered Henry, somewhat exasperated but very, very grateful nonetheless. He looked at Finch. "How are you feeling?"

"Eternally grateful, sir; you saved my life back there."

"Oh, nonsense," said Henry, turning to the goat. "Is it a bad wound, Madame?"

"I think the bullet has badly lacerated his right foreleg but passed through him, Monsieur, so he is lucky in one sense."

"Whoever did this has gone, I reckon," said Daphne. "I heard a motorbike roar off down the hill."

"Yes, indeed," said Henry, "and I recognised that purple tailcoat too. There is only one cat in the world who dresses that badly, though it'd be hard to prove it was him, of course." He turned again to Finch. "We should get you to a doctor. Would you like to rest here overnight?"

"No, sir. Let's head back to London. Madame Chèvre has done a good job of patching me up, though perhaps somebody else could drive?" said Finch, wincing a bit.

"I'll drive," said Daphne quickly. "But I think it's a good idea to bring the shotgun, just in case."

So they loaded the trunk into the car and then Madame Chèvre telephoned her neighbours, the Grigsons; a large family of meerkats who would provide some additional security at the house.

After all the excitement, the journey back to London was somewhat uneventful. Henry ended up in the back (again), as Daphne decided to drive and Finch declared (again) that he couldn't really sit in the back and be chauffeured. They arrived back in London quite late in the evening and dropped Daphne at her hotel before finally pulling up outside the flat in Eaton Square. Despite Henry's objections given Finch's injuries, the bulldog insisted that they both bring the trunk inside the flat immediately and take all precautions to protect it, locking all the doors and shuttering the windows.

That night Henry made arrangements for Dr Dixon, the Oxshott family doctor, to pay a visit and check on Finch. Dixon, an old and now somewhat overweight Labrador, had delivered Henry as a kitten all those years ago and was very close to the family. Having inspected the bulldog thoroughly, he declared him to be in no danger. He then proceeded to carefully dress the wound again before departing into the night. The two animals retired to their beds, somewhat overwhelmed by the day's events.

Chapter 10

The next week or two passed without incident. Daphne came to visit every day. At first she brought only sympathy, but after Henry's disastrous attempts to cook, she brought food and drink as well. Finch slowly recovered his health and made arrangements with a bullion dealer for the trunk to be collected and melted down into gold bars. Henry was very nervous about the whole business. He worried that it would be the last they would ever see of it. Finch assured him that the dealer in question was an old business associate of his Uncle John and, as such, would be true to his word. He also made it clear that you couldn't just walk into any old gold dealer and sell them gold without any evidence that you actually owned it. This was especially true when you were trying to sell a trunk made of solid gold that had been crafted in South America. To any normal person this would all sound quite far-fetched, and might well attract the attention of the Metropolitan Police, as well as Customs and Excise.

At the beginning of the third week, Finch was up and out of bed. He was quite restless, and told Henry that he had been waited upon for long enough and needed to keep himself busy. He therefore suggested that it was high time to clean the flat properly. On the day he arrived he had concentrated on the kitchen and the drawing room, but that still left lots to be done. One area that had particularly caught his attention was the dark hallway, which was piled up with books, leather boxes, and a vast and varied selection of sporting equipment (comprising skis, tennis racquets, squash racquets, croquet mallets, and so on). It is fair to say that all this equipment had been purchased by Henry in various bouts of enthusiasm to commence sporting activities, but had rarely been used.

So, on a Sunday morning that neither animal would ever forget, Finch commenced the cleaning operations in the hall. Henry, meanwhile, was happily perusing the newspaper, turning every now and then to stare with immense satisfaction at a large cardboard box stuffed full of used twenty-pound notes that had been delivered by the bullion dealer the day before. Then he heard a noise and looked up from his newspaper to see Finch in the doorway, ashen-faced and duster in hand.

"Sir, I think you need to come into the hall," he said.

"Finch, you look like you have had a nasty shock."

"Indeed. Can you please come quickly?"

"Righty-ho," said Henry as he jumped up from his chair. "I do hope you haven't broken one of my squash racquets!" He bounded into the hall, not knowing quite what to expect. He had never seen Finch look this way before. But nothing, just nothing, could have prepared him for what happened next.

Finch was standing at the back of the gloomy hall in front of a large Georgian chest of drawers that stood about six feet

tall. Above it, quite high off the ground and in the darkest corner, was a smallish painting of about thirty centimetres by forty. The bulldog was pointing at the painting. Henry went over and stood by him, and they looked at the painting together.

Henry then turned and looked at the bulldog. Finch slowly turned to look back at the cat. Without a word, they both then turned their gaze back to the picture.

"Finch, in the drawing room there is the postcard from my Uncle B, sitting on the chimney piece. I recall that you had the good sense to bring it with you from Yews Hall."

His companion simply nodded.

"Could you please bring it here?"

Finch disappeared into the drawing room and returned in the blink of an eye. Without a word, he handed the postcard to Henry, who, in silence, held it up to the picture on the wall and compared them. They were a perfect match. Henry then handed the postcard back to Finch. The bulldog had no need to repeat the procedure himself. As soon as he had spotted the painting hanging there in the deep recesses of the hall he knew it was a perfect match to the postcard.

"Finch, I recall that the postcard mentions the title of the painting: *The Dogana from the Steps of the Hotel Europa*. Does it also give the name of the painter?"

"Yes, it does, and I know the artist well."

"Who is it, then?"

"It's Turner. Joseph Mallord William Turner."

"Is he famous?"

"The consensus among art experts is that he is Britain's greatest ever artist."

"Blimey," said Henry. "I thought I had heard of him. Aren't there a lot of his paintings in the Tate Gallery?"

"Indeed, sir."

"So what we are looking at now," said Henry, with some deliberation and choosing his words very carefully, "is a painting by Britain's greatest ever artist."

This time Finch did not think it necessary to respond. A protracted silence followed, with both animals deep in thought. Then Henry read out loud part of the message that had been written on the postcard from Uncle B:

It is a view that I have come to love, and I hope you will enjoy it too.

There followed another long silence.

"What do we do now?" said Henry eventually.

"I suggest I make a pot of tea, sir," replied Finch.

"Excellent idea! And after that?"

"Well, I think we should carefully, very carefully, take the painting down to see if there are any other clues to this mystery. But it seems to me that your Uncle B wanted you to have this painting…"

"…and Uncle Crispin wants it too!" Henry finished the sentence.

"Yes, sir. Though what I don't quite understand is how it ended up in your Aunt Dolly's flat."

Together they moved the picture into the drawing room – both of them had forgotten about the pot of tea. Having propped it up carefully on the oxblood sofa, they stared at it again for some time.

"I think it is a jolly nice painting," Henry finally remarked. "But then, I don't know a great deal about art, as is clear from that old plate you identified as a Meissen. So tell me, Finch, is it any good, this picture? Perhaps it's just a fake?"

"No," said Finch with some passion. "This is no fake. Everything about it looks absolutely correct to me in terms of the subject, the brushwork and the use of light. Of course, we should get a Turner expert at the Tate Gallery to verify it. May I inspect the back of the painting, sir?"

"Be my guest!"

As Finch turned the picture around to reveal the back, they noticed that a small envelope was tucked behind part of the frame. Having received Henry's nodded approval to do so, Finch gently lifted the letter out and handed it to his employer. This turned out to be entirely the right thing to do, as the envelope had Henry's name written on the front.

"Finch, I really don't think I can take much more of this drama. Would you open it for me?"

Finch duly did so. "There is a letter inside. Would you like me to read it?"

"No – just throw it in the fire. Really?! Of course I want you to read the letter!" Then Henry blushed. "Oh, Finch, I am so sorry, I shouldn't have snapped at you like that. It's just… it's just…"

"Don't worry, I will read the letter."

My dear Henry,

I write to you from the banks of the Orinoco, and your Aunt Dolly will place this letter where you now find it. As you are now reading this letter, you have either discovered it by accident, or you have followed the trail that I have set for you. It doesn't really matter either way, but of course, I sincerely hope it is the latter. You know how much I love treasure hunts.

Let me begin by saying that I have decided to leave Yews Hall to a beautiful cat called Daphne because she has a wonderful dream and I believe she can fulfil it there. I am sure that you will approve. She is a very special young lady.

But it was always my intention to leave this picture to you. You know how much I hate hotels, and how much I loathe Venice. It is for those reasons that I thought you alone might guess that there was something fishy about the postcard, and that that might lead you to think there might be something of a mystery behind it. I am sure that you will be very amused when I tell you that I asked your Aunt Dolly some years back to buy me the best picture she could find on her travels in the West of England. I am convinced that she bought this painting firstly because it is a magnificent painting, but also as a way to tease me about my distaste for Venice; a city which she herself always loved. But even though it is a picture of Venice, I fell in love with it and it has become my most precious possession, which is why I have decided to leave it to you when I die. I came up with the idea of a puzzle – and therefore a bit of a treasure hunt – to make you work (at least a little bit) for your inheritance.

For many years, the painting was down at Yews Hall. It was only when your Uncle Crispin caught sight of it and guessed what it might be that I realised I needed to move it somewhere as I was very concerned that he might try to steal it. So I agreed with your Aunt Dolly that she would safeguard it for me (and you). Crispin has always been scared of her and will never go to her flat in Eaton Square, so I think it's safe there. I wrote this letter and arranged for you to receive the Bible and the postcard in the trunk so that you can follow the trail to Dolly's flat and claim your inheritance when I die. As Dolly is no doubt with you now, she will be able to verify the tale that I have told you in this letter. Please enjoy the painting.

Your loving uncle,
Bartholomew

Finch folded the letter carefully and handed it to Henry.

"Well, I suppose what Uncle B failed to predict is that Aunt Dolly would predecease him," Henry remarked.

"Yes, sir."

"And in fact, when she died and left me the entire contents of this flat, I inherited the picture anyway."

"I suppose so, yes."

"So I inherited the picture from Uncle B, but I also inherited it from Aunt D. So does that mean that I inherited it twice? Is that even possible?"

"No, sir. I think, strictly speaking, you inherited it from your Aunt Dolly, and no one, other than perhaps your Uncle Bartholomew, could challenge that. He might have argued that your aunt was only looking after it for him, but he either didn't think about what would happen if she died before him, or he thought it wouldn't change anything if she did, as from his perspective it was always going to be yours when he died."

Henry was terribly confused by all this, so he thought he might change the subject. "But do you think we would have discovered the painting anyway, even without the postcard as a clue? Sorry, let me rephrase that… Would *you* have worked out it was a Turner painting, without the postcard to prompt you?"

"I don't know. It's not every day that you find a Turner hidden at the back of a hallway."

"Correct, Finch; if it wasn't for you I would have looked at that picture every day of the week and not known what it was. It would have been just another picture, so to speak. Hidden in plain sight. Finch?" Henry continued.

"Yes, sir?"

"Would you be interested in a permanent position at 77 Eaton Square? I can offer excellent pay and conditions."

"Yes, sir, that's agreed. As long as I may propose one condition in return."

"Which is…?"

"You never, ever sell that painting."

Part Two

The Umpire Strikes Back

Chapter 1

It was dusk on a chilly evening in late September 1985. The setting was Hampstead in North London. Still regarded by its residents as a village in its own right, Hampstead is famous for its large Heath, expensive houses (many of which are hidden behind electric gates), and excellent selection of cafés, boutiques and shops. What is less well known is that, a short walk from the village at the very end of a narrow road that runs alongside the Heath, there is also a small paved area that is home to a number of caravans.

One caravan was very different from all the others located nearby. Whilst the others were quite spacious, clean and well cared for, this one was very small and dirty. Each of its four steel wheels were badly corroded though years of neglect and, when it rained, they dropped a steady stream of brown rust flakes which stained the ground beneath.

The tenant of this decrepit vehicle was a cat called Crispin Butler. He had been born many years before in a large country house deep in the Sussex countryside; a very different setting to the caravan park. Crispin was a cat of dubious character; mean-spirited and cruel to small animals. Come to think of it, he was mean to medium, large and even extra-large animals too. He never had a good word for anybody, and in return, of course, nobody had a good word for him. Not that that bothered him in the slightest. The Taylor family, a respectable clutch of chickens who lived next door, had welcomed him when he first arrived, but relations had turned sour after they caught him red-handed attempting some petty thievery on more than one occasion. He led a solitary existence.

That evening, Crispin sat at his desk on an old, wobbly pink velour chair that, like him, had seen better days. In fact, it had seen better weeks and years too. What little was left of the foam lining poked out from the worn and torn threadbare velour. The desk in front of him was a cheap children's desk made of white chipboard and, true to its name, was chipped all over and covered in dents and scratches. It was overflowing with a vast selection of crumpled papers, chewed pencils and battered paperbacks. On top of these rested not one but three ashtrays: one of marble (again chipped and covered in scratches), one of lurid green onyx (a material deemed very fashionable in the 1970s), and one bearing an incredibly badly painted seaside scene of Benidorm in Spain. Each ashtray was overflowing with cheroots; rather foul-smelling cheap cigars which Crispin joked were his "only vice". If only that were true.

Any sympathy for Crispin and his parlous circumstances would be completely misplaced. He had spent his entire life cheating friends and acquaintances out of money with promises and lies of 'get rich' schemes, or 'certain winners' at the racecourse. But he never used their money to invest or to place bets; instead he frittered it away on expensive habits and habitats. Now he owned nothing, not even a guilty conscience.

The floor of the caravan was no better than the desk. The filthy brown nylon carpet was thankfully hidden by a second carpet of old newspapers, magazines and vinyl album covers. This was a time before digital music; even CDs were a novelty in 1985. To the side of the desk, gaudy clothes were piled very high on two old tubular chrome steel chairs that were slowly rusting away at the joints. Each pile of clothes leaned inwards towards the other to a precarious degree that seemed to defy the laws of physics. Meanwhile, an unattended kettle was boiling away on a small, portable electric hob. A tin of condensed milk was open, half eaten. It could have been there a few minutes or a few days. It was hard to tell.

Crispin was oblivious to all this squalor. He was instead focused on two postcards that were propped up on the desk, side by side and leaning against a dirty, stained and chipped mug half full of cold coffee and celebrating the royal wedding of Prince Charles and Lady Diana Spencer in 1981. Like the milk, the coffee could have been there a few minutes or a few days. Again, it was hard to tell. Time stood still in the caravan.

The only source of light in the caravan was a dusty, naked light bulb, as it was now dark outside. That being said, even in daytime the brightest shaft of sunlight would have struggled to penetrate the small, dirty windows hung with thick net curtains of a dark grey colour. They had possibly been white when originally purchased in 1975, but had certainly not been washed since that date.

Crispin pick up both postcards and stared intently at them in turn with his one good eye. One postcard was a reproduction of a black-and-white photograph of a rather lovely country house, taken in around 1930. It was titled *Yews Hall, Sussex*. It was his parents' home and his birthplace; he had been delivered in the gunroom. The second postcard was a reproduction of a painting by J. M. W. Turner, the famous English landscape painter, titled *The Dogana from the Steps of the Hotel Europa*, which depicted a scene from Venice in Italy.

Crispin was convinced that these two possessions (the house and the painting – not the two postcards) rightfully belonged to him and had been stolen from him. The loss had not left Crispin slightly irritated, or a little bit cross, or pretty angry. It was worse – far worse. He was incandescent with a silent, deadly, slow-burning rage. But now he had a plan, a master plan, to recover both items and so regain what he saw as his rightful inheritance. He had lain low for many months since the reading of the will, but now he was ready to strike back. He had decided that he was the lawful owner of Yews Hall and the Turner painting, whatever anyone else thought. His campaign of retribution would begin with the recovery of the painting.

Over the years, everyone had dismissed him as a pushy upstart. To them he was just Bartholomew's sly younger brother. He'd tried to throw his weight around, but everyone joked that his only role of authority in life was as the umpire of the annual cricket match between Yews Hall and Wadhurst Cricket Club. Well now, he cackled, it was time for the umpire to strike back!

Chapter 2

That same evening, a few miles to the south, in a flat located at 77 Eaton Square in Belgravia (another fancy part of London), the aforementioned nincompoop lounged on an oxblood leather sofa. This judgement was somewhat harsh. Henry was not the cleverest of cats but he was far from stupid. His average intelligence was amply compensated by other attributes. He was very handsome, even noble in appearance. He was a considerate fellow, and possessed a very strong instinct for some things, one of which was that he was an especially good judge of character. So when Finch had turned up at his door looking for a job, Henry knew he had struck gold. Indeed, a few days after Finch's arrival Henry had struck gold literally, but that is another story, already told.

Now, six months later, the two of them had formed a strong bond. On the surface it seemed like the attraction of opposites. One was young and somewhat naive; the other was older and shaped by some tough life experiences, including active military service. The cat came from a wealthy background, whereas the bulldog had grown up in more humble surroundings and under the spell of his Uncle John, a career criminal. Nevertheless, they had much in common too, not least a passion for *Scrabble* that would see them through many long evenings.

Henry was heavily reliant on Finch in so many ways, paid him generously and treated him with the utmost respect. Finch, who was the smarter of the two, nevertheless relished his role as an employee. In his time in the Royal Tank Regiment his happiest years had been as the batman (a sort of personal servant) to the colonel commandant. He felt his role now was similar in many ways; that of a trusted assistant rather than a dogservant. He was very fond of his young employer and knew he was a kind and decent fellow, and, surprisingly, the fact that Henry was a little lazy didn't bother him at all.

Henry had, in fact, come to find his employee indispensable, and it was therefore with some trepidation that he viewed Finch's upcoming vacation. The bulldog was off to see his ailing mother, who lived near Bath. Henry had suggested that he take the car; the rather splendid brown Rolls-Royce Silver Shadow saloon. He did this partly because he knew that Finch would relish taking his mother out in it, but also in the hope that it would mean that the bulldog could return to London quickly and at short notice should the need arise.

On the Monday afternoon, as he prepared to depart, Finch fussed a little unnecessarily over Henry. He went over the menu plan he had designed for the week that he would be away. Everything was prepared and ready to cook, stored for now in the fridge or the freezer. Arrangements had been made for a team of tortoises to come in and clean every day (slowly but thoroughly), and the laundry would be taken care of by Snow White, the local dry cleaner run by a fastidious and slightly neurotic Japanese snow monkey who was the only dry cleaner that Finch trusted.

"So would you like me to run through things again, sir?" asked Finch.

"Oh really, Finch, anyone would think you were off to the Amazon for six months! I can think I can survive for a week whilst you are in Bath!" said Henry with a large grin, tugging at his whiskers before he added, somewhat nervously, "But can I just double-check that I have the correct telephone number for your mother? Just in case of an emergency."

This was in the days before mobile phones were in everyone's hands. So Finch repeated the number for the umpteenth time and Henry wrote it down (also for the umpteenth time) on a scrap of paper, so that there were now at least a dozen pieces of paper that contained the number scattered around the flat.

The fact was that they were both slightly apprehensive. This was to be the first time since they had met that they would spend time apart. Henry was concerned about how he would get on without his companion. Finch worried about the same thing. He didn't want anything untoward to happen to Henry, but on the other hand he also secretly hoped his employer would feel lost without him. Of course, they were both very English and therefore very reserved, so they didn't express their emotions openly as Finch prepared to leave, preferring instead to rely on a firm pawshake before the bulldog slowly walked up the steps from the front door of the flat and loaded his kitbag into the boot of the Rolls-Royce. Henry quietly closed the front door and walked slowly back down the poorly lit hall, feeling a little lost.

Chapter 3

The first few days passed without incident. On the Wednesday morning, the telephone rang.

"Henry?"

"Daphne! How lovely to hear from you! How are you? How are things down at the hall?"

"I am very well, thank you, and everything is running smoothly here. And you?"

"Surviving. Finch is away seeing his mother in Bath. He's gone for a week. He left on Monday."

Daphne giggled. "Have you eaten since then?"

"Yes I have, but thank you for asking," replied Henry, sensing that he was being teased, but maintaining his good temper.

"Sausage Surprise every night?" Daphne giggled again. She was teasing him because she knew, and he knew that she knew, that he was the worst cook for some miles around, and in central London that encompassed several million people. Sausages cooked in the oven with tomato and beans was the only dish he could prepare that would scrape a grade of 'Adequate' in any basic cooking-school exam. So it had soon earned the nickname of 'Sausage Surprise' amongst

Henry's friends because if he invited you round for supper and mentioned that he was the chef, there was no surprise as to what you would be eating that night.

Henry continued to take the teasing in good humour as he responded. "Actually, Finch prepared a week's worth of provisions for me, so I am well fed and watered, and sausage free. I have also popped out every now and then for supper," he admitted quietly.

"Well, I am up in town tomorrow night, and I would like to take you to dinner somewhere nice. What do you fancy?"

"Oh, that's very kind of you. How about Wiltons on Jermyn Street? Best seafood in town."

"Sounds lovely. Can you book it for 7pm? I don't like to eat too late."

"Any particular reason for popping up to town?" inquired Henry, trying to strike the balance between polite curiosity and nosiness.

"You," said Daphne, and she put the telephone down before Henry could respond.

He felt wonderful. Daphne was not only very beautiful, but terribly clever. Time spent with her was always time well spent indeed. She was coming up to London because she wanted to see him. *How nice*, he thought to himself as he sauntered into the kitchen and took out one of Finch's ready meals from the freezer.

Only when he was halfway through supper did the slightly unsettling thought occur to him that maybe Daphne's visit to London had some ulterior motive. Without Finch's brains to rely on he felt somewhat anxious, and tugged his whiskers repeatedly. He didn't sleep well that night.

Chapter 4

He left the flat around 6.30 the next evening and decided to stroll to the restaurant, meandering past Buckingham Palace and through Green Park to get there. Wiltons was indeed one of the finest fish restaurants in the capital. It had opened in 1742 and, in their own words, 'been synonymous for the finest oysters, wild fish and game and traditional, courteous, hospitality'. They also happened to have an excellent wine list. So when Henry settled down at his regular table just before 7pm with a glass of vintage champagne, his mood lifted. After all, what was he worrying about? It would be nice to see Daphne for the first time since the early summer.

She had been hidden down at Yews Hall, working, she declared, on her dream, and had banned Henry from visiting for the time being. To him it all seemed a bit mysterious, and he had complained to Finch that it was a tad strange for her to deprive him not only of the chance to visit Yews Hall, but also of the joy of her company. Finch, ever the voice of wisdom, had explained that whatever Daphne was up to, it had the blessing of Uncle

Bartholomew. When he left Yews Hall and the surrounding land to her in his will, Uncle B had specifically mentioned that it was to allow Daphne to fulfil her dream there, and the sagacious bulldog was happy to rely upon that. If it was good enough for Uncle B, it was good enough for Henry too, they both agreed.

Daphne arrived a little after 7pm. The diners who lined her route fell silent as she made her way to Henry's table. Dressed in a simple cream silk outfit and a single (albeit rather large) diamond pendant which sparkled in the soft candlelight, she rather took their breath away.

"Daphne, you look wonderful!" exclaimed Henry as he rose to greet her.

She gave him a soft kiss on the cheek. "Thank you, Henry; it's been too long since we saw each other and I know it's my fault. But I will get straight to the point. Tonight I am finally ready to tell you about my dream for Yews Hall."

"Splendid! Champagne?"

"Well, maybe just half a glass," she said as she took the menu proffered by the young squirrel waitress and began to peruse it. "What's good here, Henry?"

"I am planning to go for smoked salmon to start, and then follow that with Dover sole."

"Sounds delicious. I will have the same, please."

Benson, the silver fox who had been Wiltons' head waiter for some years now, had silently appeared at their table to take the order, and nodded his approval. "May I suggest a selection of seasonal green vegetables and new potatoes, ma'am?" he added as he scribbled down the order on a small notepad with his silver pencil, finishing with a flourish. This was only for dramatic effect, though, as he had committed the order to memory already.

Daphne nodded and off the fox trotted, satisfied, dancing ever so slightly. A perfect foxtrot, in fact.

"Don't keep me in suspense then, Daphne!" continued Henry when they had the table to themselves again.

"Mmmm?"

"What is your dream?"

"Mice," she purred, looking at the pale straw-coloured liquid in her glass before continuing.

"What?"

"Mice and other small rodents."

"What, are you breeding them? To eat?"

"No! Henry, how could you think such a thing?" Daphne looked offended.

"Apologies." He straightened his jacket, wiped his whiskers with his napkin and pulled a serious expression before continuing. "Daphne, tell me about your dream."

"Well, you know all the land surrounding Yews Hall?"

"Yes, I am familiar with the place. but I have been banned from visiting for some months now."

"That's where I'm going to be making my dream a reality. A mouse sanctuary."

Her companion just shook his head as (not for the first time) he was completely lost.

"Henry, I am going to create an orphanage for mice and other small rodents who've been abandoned, left alone and homeless."

Henry was lost for words. He didn't have a strong view on mice, so he wasn't sure quite what to say. Instead he stared blankly for a few moments at the beautiful cat opposite before she continued.

"It's going to take at least two years before we can build all the facilities and get things up and running, so I wanted to be sure before I got everyone all excited about it. Anyway, it's full speed ahead now but, before I do it, I wanted to seek your permission for something. Hence our dinner date."

"Why ask me? It's your house now, and Uncle B clearly had every faith in you."

"Yes, but there is a small catch. There always is, isn't there? I will need some working capital to pay the animals who will help me build the dormitories and the hospital, and to buy all the other bits I need for a sanctuary. Believe me, there is so much of it! I have some income from the farmland but I need a bit more; quite a lot more, in fact. So," here she hesitated a bit and looked at Henry coyly over her glass, "I have had an offer from someone who wants to buy two acres to the far south of the plot, on the other side of the valley. They are offering almost five hundred thousand pounds an acre, so it's a big amount. But it means selling some of the estate, and I just want your blessing. It's important to me that you approve. The solicitors from London who would act on the sale tell me that the family has owned the land there since 1740! The only living member of the Butler family is your Uncle Crispin, or 'Umpire Crispin' as they call him in the village, and no one has a good word for him, so his blessing doesn't count for much. But I know the villagers love you, and your mother was a Butler too! So, Henry Oxshott, do you approve?"

"Of course I do, provided I can visit soon!" He grinned.

"That's a deal," said Daphne as she raised her glass to Henry's, her aquamarine eyes dazzling him in the soft candlelight. "To Yews Hall!"

"To the sanctuary!"

The remainder of the dinner passed off very well as the two cats caught up on news and shared stories. Daphne was always a little reticent, though, when asked about her childhood, her parents and even the time she had spent with Uncle B, deftly changing the subject whenever it came up. Henry was too polite to pry, so they spent most of the time talking about his relatives and life at Yews Hall in the 1970s. At around nine o'clock Daphne announced that she planned to return to Sussex that night, and despite Henry's protestations she was resolute. He saw her outside to her black Land Rover Defender parked nearby and bid her farewell, feeling slight downcast as she drove away that, after a delightful couple of hours, this feline ray of sunshine was gone again from his life.

Chapter 5

The next morning, the doorbell rang just before nine. Unusually, Henry was up and out of bed. He nevertheless remained in his usual spot on the sofa for the first two rings before he remembered that Finch was still away, and so eventually made his way down the hall to open the door himself. There, standing in front of him, was a spotted hyena wearing a rather threadbare pinstriped suit. A faded brown trilby was perched awkwardly on his head. He was carrying a rather large carpetbag with a worn leather handle. Henry's hackles went up and he arched his back ever so slightly.

"Mr Oxshott, sir? I am Anthony Briggs from the Tate Gallery. Mr Finch asked me to pop round to inspect your wonderful painting."

Henry relaxed slightly, though he still wasn't entirely happy. "Finch spoke to you, you say?"

"Yes, is he in?"

"No, he's away at the moment."

"Oh, that's a shame. Maybe I got my dates mixed up. I will come back when he is here. Such a shame. I was so keen to verify the authenticity of your Turner. What a rare find!"

"Well, if Finch spoke to you, you should come in. I am the owner of this flat," said Henry, slightly irritated that this fellow Briggs seemed to suggest that he would only deal with Finch. As though Henry were a child left at home whilst his parents were out!

"Very good, sir," replied the hyena as he entered the flat, ostentatiously wiping his feet for ten seconds whilst taking a good look around.

He then followed Henry to the back of the gloomy hall to inspect the picture in question, which was in a dark corner above a large antique chest of drawers.

"I say, sir, what a beauty! Can we get it down so I can take a proper look, move it into the light – perhaps in the drawing room?"

Henry acquiesced and the two of them carried the small picture into the drawing room and set it upon the oxblood leather sofa. The hyena stood back and then slowly sat down on his hind legs, staring approvingly at the picture in silence for a few moments. He then turned to Henry.

"It's a little forward of me, I know, sir, but is there any chance of a cup of tea? I have come straight from home and it was a bit of an early start."

"Well, yes, very good, let me see what I can do," said Henry. He was a little taken aback by the request, especially coming from a hyena wearing a brown trilby, but his good breeding prevailed.

"Milk and four sugars, please!" shouted his guest as Henry disappeared into the kitchen, leaving the hyena alone with the Turner.

Henry spent quite some time trying to find a cup, a saucer, a spoon, the tea, the milk and the sugar whilst he waited for the kettle to boil, which seemed to take forever. When he finally emerged from the kitchen with the cup of tea, he was somewhat surprised to see that Mr Briggs had one foot out of the front door.

"All good, sir! I put it back, don't worry! I'll write you something confirming that it's an original Turner when I get back to the Tate. Good day to you!" And with that he was off, leaving Henry to shake his head wearily.

He did take the trouble to look back down the dark hall and saw the picture restored to its proper place, so he strolled back into the drawing room.

What a funny chap! he thought to himself before plonking back down on the sofa, where he then proceeded to drink the cup of tea he was holding, wincing slightly at the sweetness of it.

Chapter 6

Finch arrived back from Bath late on Sunday evening. He unloaded his kitbag from the Rolls-Royce and greeted his employer warmly. He had missed him, and was pleased to be back at 77 Eaton Square. Henry had already eaten one of the meals that Finch had prepared for him and washed it down with half a bottle of Beaujolais, so was feeling that all was well with the world. As the bulldog unpacked in his room, Henry stood outside in the hall, chatting to him and relaying the news about his dinner with Daphne and her plans for Yews Hall. Finch was suitably impressed and agreed that it showed great enterprise, albeit quite challenging to start something like that from scratch. The conversation then turned to the visit from the hyena.

"Oh yes, and your fellow Briggs from the Tate dropped by on Friday morning."

"Pardon, sir?"

"Mr Briggs came by to look at the Turner. Said he was sorry to have missed you, must have been a mix-up on the date."

"Are you saying someone called Briggs came by, claiming to be from the Tate and to know me?"

"Yes," said Henry. A sinking sensation crept slowly through all four of his legs, and then came a swirling feeling in his stomach.

"Can you describe him?" Finch fixed the cat with a rather piercing stare that he saved for special occasions, which only made Henry feel worse.

"Well, he was a spotted hyena. He wore a rather shabby suit and carried a large carpetbag. On his head he wore a—"

"—faded brown trilby," interrupted Finch as he completed the description.

"So you do know him?" gulped Henry, not sure if that was good news or bad news at this point, but sensing that the direction of travel was towards the 'bad' end of the spectrum.

"Yes, sir. Buster Briggs of Bethnal Green. A devious fellow who once tried, and failed, to cheat my Uncle John. You didn't let him near the painting, did you?"

"Well, I helped him to get it down so he could take a better look at it in the light in the drawing room. But don't worry. He put it back and then just headed off."

"Helped him to get it down..." repeated Finch quietly to himself from between gritted canines as he marched swiftly out of the room and turned into the hall towards the picture. He had a thunderous look on his face.

Henry stared at him sheepishly.

"Did you, at any time, leave Briggs alone with the Turner?"

"Only when I went to make a cup of tea."

"It was Briggs that asked you to make a cup of tea, wasn't it, sir?"

"Yes," Henry replied quietly. "How did you know that?"

"It's one of his trademark scams, I am afraid. Gives him time alone."

"But the picture, the Turner, it's still there. He put it back."

Finch managed to get the painting down from the wall on his own and took it into the drawing room. He barely looked at it before he turned to Henry and declared, "This is a copy, sir. And a poor one at that." He growled ominously.

A pregnant silence was followed by a laboured pause before it eventually gave birth to a confession.

"I have messed up badly, haven't I, Finch?" offered Henry weakly.

The bulldog had by now calmed down. He had mentally replayed the events described by his employer and so had a very good idea of what had happened. His anger was now directed elsewhere, and he felt the need to console Henry. "Well, it's not your fault. Buster Briggs is one of the best in the business. He is a skilled and confident trickster. Whilst you were out in the kitchen making the cup of tea, he took out the fake copy of the painting from his carpetbag and switched it with the real one. He then put the real one in his bag and hung the fake one on the wall. The whole thing would have taken him no more than thirty seconds. But what puzzles me is that he would not have known about the Turner without a tip-off from someone. Those tortoises that came in to clean – can you vouch for them?"

"Yes, they worked for Aunt Dolly for many years; they're semi-retired now. Never a suggestion that they stole anything from the flat in all that time."

Finch scratched his ear repeatedly with his hind leg. He always did that when he was deep in thought. "It's Crispin Butler. He must be behind it."

"Uncle Crispin? Really?"

"I am sure of it, sir. He just used Briggs to do his dirty work."

"You think so? But how did Briggs know you were in Bath?"

"What time did he turn up? Around nine in the morning?"

"Yes, that's right."

"Well, as you know, that's when I am usually out running errands. The fact that I was in Bath was only a coincidence, so it made no difference."

"But he asked for you, Finch."

"Yes, just to see if I was in. If I had been, he would have scarpered."

"Well, I suppose Uncle C worked out that the painting must be either in this flat or in some bank vault, so it was only a matter of time before he came looking."

"He has probably had the place under surveillance for some time now, observing our routine. Which is how he knew that nine in the morning would be a good time to strike."

Another silence followed.

"What do we do now, Finch?"

"It's very simple. We get the painting back."

"But it could be anywhere by now. I don't even know where Uncle C lives."

"OK, leave this to me. Can I suggest that you go down to Yews Hall? Crispin may have plans to strike there too. If anyone odd turns up, just alert me. I would tell Daphne to get the Grigsons back for extra security. In the meantime, I need to reach out to a few old friends of my Uncle John. Probably best if you aren't around for that, sir." Finch gave Henry another piercing look.

"As you wish. I will telephone Daphne tomorrow and say that I would like to go down sometime in the next week. She did say at dinner that I'm welcome to stay any time for as long as I like. I will leave you to have full use of the Silver Shadow. I don't feel much like driving anyway."

With that the two animals retired to bed, one feeling very foolish and one feeling very angry. It was not the homecoming that either had expected.

Chapter 7

Just after midnight, a hyena sat on a bench overlooking the River Thames near Temple Underground Station. It was a cloudless night and the moon shone brightly, reflected in the silent, lapping waters beneath. Buster had with him a carpetbag that contained a rather valuable painting, though he didn't realise how valuable. He had a rendezvous with a client, and was feeling very tired. Indeed, he must have dozed off for a bit, as he awoke to find a long cat sitting right next to him, wheezing slightly.

"Did you get it, Briggs?"

"Oh, indeed, sir. A piece of cake. No sign of the bulldog, just like you said. Just the young cat. Putty in my hands, he was! Like taking candy from a small kid! Almost felt sorry for him, I did; seemed like a good kitten."

"Good," purred Crispin. "Well done, laddie. I assume the painting's in the bag?"

"Yeah. So where's my fee then, guv'nor?"

"All in good time. I need to sell the picture first."

"That's not what you told me! You said ten thousand pounds cash on delivery."

"Well, maybe circumstances have changed. What are you going to do – report me to the police for not paying you for a stolen painting?"

"Circumstances have changed, have they? Really? Or maybe you are just a lying toerag." The hyena raised his voice.

Crispin grabbed the bag and ran across the road, shouting as he went that the hyena needn't worry and that he would get his money.

Buster glowered after him. He knew a thief and a liar when he saw one. "No one crosses Buster Briggs and gets away with it," he muttered to himself.

Chapter 8

Henry set off for Charing Cross Station the next afternoon, his suitcase in his hand. He had telephoned Daphne in the morning and explained that, as he had some time on his hands, he thought it would be rather nice to head down to Yews Hall. She was delighted and suggested that he come down that afternoon, not least because the following morning the team would start the building work for the infirmary and storage buildings for the sanctuary.

On arriving at the station, Henry made his way to the ticket office. In the short queue he was able to make out two counters open for ticket sales: one occupied by a red squirrel, the epitome of bustle and efficiency; the other by an overweight panda who sat silently munching on some bamboo. Although Henry hoped that he would be served by the squirrel, inevitably when it was his turn he was summoned by the panda with the merest suggestion of a wave forward. The thick glass partition made conversation difficult as the sound was somewhat muffled.

"Yes?" the panda mumbled before leaning back again, clearly exhausted. After that he yawned four times and

stretched ever so slightly before slouching back down again on a swivel chair that was far too small for him.

"Good morning. I would like a ticket to Wadhurst, please."

"Watford?"

"No, Wadhurst."

"Haven't heard of that one. Wait a moment." The panda then very, very slowly proceeded to consult a large directory that contained every single train station in the United Kingdom. "You are at the wrong station. You need to go to Kings Cross and change at Retford, or go from St Pancras and change at Sheffield. Next customer, please."

"Nonsense; I always go from here. Why would I want to get to the South of England from a station in North London and via Yorkshire?" Henry was starting to get exasperated.

The panda remained silent for quite some time. He appeared nonplussed, and chewed on a small piece of bamboo whilst he looked thoughtfully at Henry. He then pointed to a sign promising that the railway company would prosecute those who used offensive language or threatening behaviour to employees of the railway.

"Are you sure you have the right station?" Henry asked.

"I am sure that you have the *wrong* station," the panda eventually responded with a smug grin.

"Look, Wadhurst is in Sussex, not Yorkshire. I don't think the redrawing of the county boundaries a few years ago made that much of a difference."

"You said Woodhouse, not Wadhurst. Woodhouse is in Yorkshire," replied the panda, tapping at the directory of train stations with his claw.

"No I did not."

"Yes you did."

"Didn't."

"Did."

Since negotiations had become deadlocked, Henry paused for thought. "OK, I have changed my mind. I no longer wish to go to Woodhouse. Instead I would like a ticket to Wadhurst in Sussex, please."

"Certainly, sir," said the panda, pleased with his victory in this epic battle of wills. "Single or return?"

"I assume a single is cheaper?"

"Not necessarily." That was all the panda said as he munched slowly on his bamboo. He was not about to impart his expert knowledge of the complex fare-ticketing system that easily.

"What is the cheapest return, then?"

"One purchased with a Student Railcard."

"I am not a student."

"Well, you should have said so."

"Is there another discount available?"

"Do you have an HM Forces, Senior Citizen or Disabled Person's Railcard?"

"No."

"Then there is the Group Saver Special, for parties of three to nine."

"I am travelling alone."

"How about Advance Purchase?"

"Yes, that sounds good. I will take that, please."

"Must be booked twelve weeks in advance."

"I want to leave before that."

"We have the Off-Peak Return. Or even better, the Super Off-Peak Return."

"OK, I will take that then, please."

"You have to travel before 9.30 in the morning."

"It's now 10.15 and I wish to travel today."

"Anytime Day Return is your best bet."

"Alright, that one then."

"Need to return today, of course."

Henry sighed heavily and looked pointedly at the panda, who just stared back at him as he munched on yet another bamboo shoot. The cat wondered where in the station they stored all the bamboo to get this panda through a single day. Then, as his thoughts slowly returned to the matter in hand, an idea came to him.

"What is the most expensive ticket that I can purchase?"

"First-Class Unlimited Travel."

"And that will allow me to take a train to Wadhurst sometime today and return whenever I like?"

"Subject to certain limited exceptions and conditions, yes."

"I will take that one then, please."

"OK. I will have to do a manual calculation for the price of that one. Nobody has ever asked me for that in all the time I have been here."

The panda then licked his paw and flicked through a large, thick book containing every possible fare price. After several minutes (but it felt like hours) he commenced typing on his computer and then finally told Henry the price of the ticket – an astronomical number. Since Henry was past caring by this stage and keen to leave Charing Cross at some point before the end of the universe in a few billion years, he handed over a large wad of pound notes and finally received his ticket. He turned to check the departure board for the next train to Wadhurst, which thankfully turned out to be leaving in fifteen minutes.

"Have a pleasant journey, sir," said the panda as Henry departed, before swiftly pulling down the white blind at his counter that had the words 'COUNTER CLOSED' printed on it in bold black letters. That marked the end of his shift and it was the quickest he had moved that day, or any other day for that matter.

Chapter 9

Whilst Henry was en route to Sussex, Finch was also busy. He had convened what he described as a "council of war" at 77 Eaton Square, with four other dogs in attendance. First, a pair of very vicious-looking black-and-tan Rottweilers called Mick and Rick, known collectively as the Turner twins. Each had a selection of nasty scars on his body, and one had an ear missing. They were not the sort of dog you wanted to upset. Next there was a silver-fawn English Mastiff known simply as Bouncer, who weighed around ninety-five kilos and took up an awful lot of space wherever he was. The fourth was a gold-and-cream long-haired Afghan hound who did look somewhat out of place in the company of these tough-looking guys. But Maggie was not your typical Afghan; she was known as one of the best fences in the business, a dog who could wheel and deal in all sorts of contraband and stolen goods. All four guests had at various times dealt with Finch's Uncle John and had known the bulldog since he was a puppy. They respected the fact that he had not followed in his uncle's footsteps and had instead joined the Royal Tank Regiment. He had kept in contact with them over the years,

and had now decided that, in the case of the stolen Turner, their help could be invaluable.

Whilst Finch made a pot of tea, the others took in the contents of the flat and teased him about how he had really landed on his feet in "posh old Eaton Square". They then turned to business. Finch gave a brief background on his employer Henry Oxshott and how he had come by the Turner painting, the history of Yews Hall, and the Butlers, Bartholomew and Crispin. He then went over the events surrounding the theft of the original picture by Buster Briggs. He sat back and sipped his tea as he invited his guests to give their views.

"Any ideas on this one? Maggie, has there been any word on the street about a stolen Turner?"

"No, love. For a job this big, usually someone knows something and then goes and tells someone else in strict confidence, and ten minutes after that the whole world knows. Not this time, though. I haven't heard sweet nothing."

Finch nodded, then looked at Bouncer, who, being a dog of few words, simply shook his head.

Mick Butler raised a paw. He didn't want to interrupt Finch. These dogs were hard and often cruel, but not rude in polite company, and this was the politest company they knew.

"Go on, Mick," encouraged the bulldog.

"Well, seems like me and Rick should catch up with old Buster. He is usually to be found in one of the pubs on Bethnal Green Road with a pint of beer in his hand. We could take him outside and have a quiet chat, so to speak."

"Thanks, Mick, but we need to tread carefully; no rough stuff unless absolutely necessary. I don't want Henry's good name dragged into this. He's a good kitten. The world of Buster Briggs is not his world, if you know what I mean."

"You are fond of him, aren't you?" said Maggie.

"Well, as I told you, he saved my life when I got shot in the leg. If he hadn't dragged me to safety, the second bullet would have killed me. I'm pretty sure that was also the work of his Uncle Crispin, so you could say it's getting a bit personal between him and me."

"How about this?" Maggie suggested. "Let's keep Mick and Rick in reserve on this one. Why don't I buy Buster a drink or two and try and find out what I can?"

"Yeah, Maggie, he won't be able to resist your charms! He's bound to let something slip about the whereabouts of the painting," said Rick.

Bouncer nodded his approval, and the others followed suit in unison. All four guests looked at Finch.

"That's agreed, then," said the bulldog. "Let's see what Maggie can find out first before we take it further with the twins. Thanks, all of you. I really appreciate this."

There was a murmur of approval from all his guests and then, with the sole item of business on the agenda satisfactorily concluded, the conversation turned to ancient history as Finch pulled out a bottle of single-malt whisky from a plastic bag and they all toasted their past endeavours, good and bad, their successes and failures, and the long list of life experiences that bound them all together.

Chapter 10

Meanwhile, Henry arrived safely in Wadhurst. The train on which he had travelled had no first-class compartment, so it ended up being the most expensive ticket ever purchased for the relatively fast trip from Charing Cross to Wadhurst. But Henry didn't mind. He was excited to see Yews Hall again for the first time since the summer. Indeed, he had only visited twice since Daphne had inherited it six months ago from Uncle Bartholomew. Daphne picked Henry up from the station in her black Land Rover Defender. He deposited his suitcase in the back and then climbed into the front passenger seat, to a deafening noise coming from the car's music system.

"Hello, Daphne. What is that racket?"

"It's the Beastie Boys."

"Is it supposed to be music?"

"Yes – it's hip-hop, from New York City!"

Henry said nothing. His musical tastes ran more to light classical and easy listening. Often when he was in an elevator he turned to the other occupants to remark upon the nice music that was playing. He did start to tap his foot to the beat, though, as they pulled out of the station car park and headed for the hall, which was only about ten minutes away by car.

"How is my favourite sanctuary owner, then?" he asked, trying to make himself heard above the music.

"Very well. How many sanctuary owners do you know?" replied the driver with a twinkle of her deep blue-green eyes.

Henry pretended to count on his paws. "You mean including you?" he asked, and she nodded in return. "One."

Daphne grinned and said nothing, but leaned over and gave Henry's paw a squeeze, which always made him feel slightly giddy. The two then drove the remainder of the short journey in silence, but a silence that was enjoyable rather than awkward.

Madame Chèvre was there to greet them as they arrived at Yews Hall. As Daphne had correctly ascertained, she was, like almost everyone else who lived in the village, very fond of Henry. He had been a polite and respectful kitten, and the fact that he was handsome, even noble, helped his standing in the community too. On top of this, the event that had established him once and for all had been when he saved the lives of two young meerkats, Keith and Charlie Grigson, who had got into difficulty in the stream that ran through the land at the hall. Cats, as you may know, do not like water. But in this case, a brave kitten dragged the two meerkats to safety and then went for help. He was even given a 'local hero' award by the mayor and presented with a small medal on a blue-and-red silk ribbon, which he still has to this day.

The two cats sat down to an early supper in the small dining room, commencing with poached salmon and French beans, followed by home-made vanilla ice cream. After they had finished, Daphne rolled out some large maps of the land at Yews Hall. She explained the detailed plans for the sanctuary, which involved showing Henry lots of drawings pinpointing the position of various buildings and all the other facilities. He tried to keep up, and nodded enthusiastically even when he had no idea what she was talking about. He only gathered that looking after small rodents seemed to be a very expensive and complicated process, and much dependent on other factors to make it a success.

"Well, it all sounds like an enormous amount of work. How are you going to hire enough people to help you?" asked Henry.

"Well, you know there are so many natural predators for rodents?"

"Right."

"I have offered them a salary if they help out and don't eat any of them."

"Very smart, Daphne. But why did you keep it a secret for so long?"

"I wanted to make sure it could be done. Bartholomew was convinced there was a real need, and that is the key to the whole thing. Otherwise it's never going to be a success, however much money and effort we all put in."

Henry looked pensive. "So you are going to need a good name for it. It's got to be very classy and clearly English. A name that evokes history and tradition.

"Any ideas, then?" Daphne asked with a smile.

"Mouse Pad."

"Pardon?"

"Mouse Pad."

"Henry, seriously, it sounds like a... I don't know what! You said 'classy'."

"Rodent Rest Home?"

"Now you are just trying to annoy me," she said, but a smile played on her face.

"Daphne's Delightful Rodent Rendezvous?"

"Stop it!" she cried, but she was laughing now.

Henry sat deep in thought for some time, then smiled brightly. "Got it!"

"Go on then," said his companion, expecting another silly name.

"Bless This Mouse!"

"Bless This Mouse..." she repeated slowly to herself.

Henry looked at Daphne with some trepidation as she walked towards him, fixing him with a steely gaze from those eyes. Before he knew it, she had kissed him on the cheek.

"Perfect, Henry. You have just named my sanctuary for me."

Chapter 11

Strange as it may seem, it was a few days later, one morning at breakfast as he piled into a large bowl of milk and cornflakes, that Henry got round to telling the story of the theft of the painting. This delay was mainly out of sheer embarrassment at his own gullibility, but also he didn't want to spoil the mood at the hall. Daphne was incensed at the news, though, like Finch, she chose not to direct her anger at Henry.

"If Uncle Crispin really is the one behind this then he is the lowest of the low. I never want to see him again," she declared with some vehemence as she vigorously spread some marmalade on her toasted sourdough.

Madame Chèvre popped her head round the door to the breakfast room and bid them good morning. She said that she had come to check that there was enough food for them both. Henry and Daphne's eyes drifted towards the sideboard that was laden with cereals, eggs (boiled and scrambled), ham, smoked salmon, and a selection of breads, cakes and pastries. They simply smiled at each other as there was enough for twenty cats, let alone two. Then in the distance the house telephone rang, and the goat disappeared to go and answer it. She returned shortly to explain that it was Finch on the line for Monsieur Oxshott. Henry took the call in the library, which had the nearest telephone to the breakfast room.

"Henry Oxshott speaking."

"Finch here. I trust all is well at the hall."

"Yes, thank you. I spoke to the Grigsons and they are providing some extra security as you suggested. No sign of Uncle C here. Any news at your end?"

"Yes, sir. Some important developments; best not to discuss over the telephone. Would you like me to come down and pick you up?"

"Yes please, Finch. I don't have the energy – or indeed the cash – to purchase another train ticket for a while."

"When would you like me to come down?"

"Tomorrow; say, around 11am?"

"Perfect. See you then. Goodbye."

"Goodbye, Finch."

Chapter 12

Finch arrived on time the following morning. Henry, who happened to be lying by the front door enjoying some late autumn sunshine, was pleased to see the brown Rolls-Royce come down the long driveway from the main road and slowly crunch across the gravel as it pulled up to the house. Daphne came out to welcome the bulldog and chatted with him for some minutes before introducing him to Jack Grigson, patriarch of the Grigson family and father of the two meerkats Henry had saved. Jack, like Finch, was ex-Army, latterly from a unit that specialised in reconnaissance behind enemy lines, and desert warfare. The bulldog and the meerkat then proceeded to tour the estate on the pretext of a security review, though most of the time was spent sharing stories of their days in the forces, as Finch was already very confident, based on his brief chat with Grigson, that the hall's security would be top-notch.

Daphne invited the bulldog to join for lunch. Madame Chèvre was an exceptional cook. (Well, she was French, after all.) All three enjoyed the roast chicken with lemon and tarragon, followed by lemon cheesecake. As they finished the meal, the hostess asked Finch to update them on developments in relation to the painting. The bulldog was taciturn at first and explained that it was a murky business and he didn't want to get either of them too involved, especially Daphne. But with some cajoling, he finally opened up.

"Well, sir, ma'am, as you know, I have some useful connections in London, some of whom know Buster Briggs. One of my contacts – a lady, in fact, called Maggie – managed to track him down in one of his regular haunts; a pub on Bethnal Green Road. He was, after a couple of pints of beer, surprisingly loquacious, not least because the person who instructed him to steal the painting has yet to pay him, despite having promised him ten thousand pounds to do the job."

"When thieves fall out, eh, Finch?" exclaimed Henry, rubbing his paws together.

"Indeed. Briggs even offered to help steal the painting back, but I think the fewer people involved the better at this stage."

"Was Crispin behind it?" asked Daphne.

Finch merely nodded before continuing. "The good news is that Briggs also tipped Maggie off as to Crispin's whereabouts. Apparently he has for some time now been renting a caravan up in Hampstead, by the Heath. It's easy to work out which one it is, too, as it's very dirty and run-down, whilst all the others are clean and well cared for."

"What's the plan then, Finch?"

"Well, two of the lads, Rick and Mick Turner, have had the place under surveillance for a couple of days now. I spoke to them before I left this morning. They got their nephew Dale to knock on the door yesterday, claiming he was selling raffle tickets for charity. Crispin opened the door about half an inch and just told him to go away, though what he actually said was very rude indeed. Dale tried to steal a look inside the caravan but he said all he could see was mess everywhere, and it was quite dark. He did hear a strange hissing noise, but that was it. Since then, Crispin has not left the property and just gets milk and pizza delivered twice a day."

"So it's going to be difficult to get a proper look in the caravan, then?" asked Henry.

"Yes; I don't think we can risk another pretext for a knock on the door as he is obviously very shifty and suspicious. What we need to do is get him out of that caravan somehow."

"Should I try and find an excuse to meet with him?" asked Henry, though he shuddered at the thought.

"No, sir; I think Crispin will suspect a ruse if you try and meet him. He will guess that you know that the painting has been stolen, and that he is the prime suspect."

"Leave it to me," said Daphne.

"What?" cried Henry. "No way! It's too dangerous."

"I agree, ma'am," said Finch.

"Look," said Daphne, "it's very simple. I invite him to dinner – Wiltons again, perhaps, or another swanky, busy restaurant. I say I have something important to tell him. Surely he will be curious, and won't turn down a free meal if he has been surviving on milk and pizza all week?"

Finch scratched his ear again with his hind leg, deep in thought. "Well, it is a good plan," he admitted at last. "It should allow us an hour or two to check over the caravan, and it gives Daphne a perfect alibi too."

"Daphne, are you sure?" Henry looked concerned. "It's going to be an awful couple of hours for you in his company. And he might try and abduct you or something."

"I am aware of that. But needs must."

"No," Henry replied, "I don't like it. I feel like we are taking advantage of you."

"OK, listen to me. You know that I will do this for you anyway, but if it makes you happier I will ask a favour in return. I won't tell you what it is just now; only once this is all out of the way, so to speak. It's quite complicated."

"It will be my honour to help in any way I can, favour owing or not. Finch, are you on board?"

"Of course, sir, ma'am."

"Right then," said the owner of Yews Hall, looking at the remains of their lunch for inspiration, "let us proceed with Operation Cheesecake."

Chapter 13

Henry and Finch departed for London immediately afterwards. Both were reluctant to leave Yews Hall but agreed that they needed to move forward swiftly with their plan. Following Henry's suggestion, later that evening Daphne telephoned and left a message for Crispin at The Kit-Kat Club, a drinking club (of which he was a life member) situated at the end of the New King's Road in Chelsea. The plan worked as Crispin rang back within an hour, so the message had obviously been passed on to him promptly. Daphne agreed to meet him the following evening for dinner, at eight o'clock at Wiltons. Crispin tried to pump her for information about her motive for the dinner, but she remained steadfast and told him he would have to wait. He was extremely sceptical and suspicious, but the lure of grilled seafood, vintage champagne and the company of such a glamourous cat prevailed.

The next day, Finch was busy making preparations. The Turner twins had been at the caravan park from sunrise, keeping tabs on Crispin (otherwise referred to as "the suspect") and the caravan ("the target vehicle"). Finch telephoned Bouncer and arranged to meet him there. He also placed a call to an elderly mongoose called Linton, whose specialist skills he thought might come in useful that evening. The bulldog made it very clear to Bouncer and Linton that they should arrive at eight o'clock and no earlier. He was keen to avoid having lots of strangers milling around the caravan park before Crispin left around 7.30 for his appointment with Daphne.

Henry wasn't quite sure how he could help, so kept out of his companion's way for most of the day. Around two o'clock in the afternoon, he popped out to Harrods to buy some clothes.

Just after 7pm, Finch announced that he was on his way up to Hampstead. He could not, of course, forbid Henry to accompany him, but he really didn't want his employer around; firstly in order to distance him from any criminal activity, and secondly because he thought that this was a job for professionals. So he was rather surprised to see Henry emerge from his bedroom dressed all in black, wearing a black balaclava and with a smudge of black boot polish on his face. So surprised, in fact, that he barely managed to stifle a huge guffaw before successfully disguising it as a coughing fit.

"Are you planning to go out, sir?" he managed to ask eventually, all the time wishing he had a camera.

"Indeed, Finch, I am ready for Operation Cheesecake."

"Your outfit is quite striking."

"Well, I thought I should get into character."

"As what exactly, sir?"

"A cat burglar. Isn't it obvious?"

"Sir, I really think you should hold the fort here. No need for you to make the trip to Hampstead."

"It's time for me to make amends for losing the painting, and I must play some role in this."

The bulldog tried to give Henry his trademark stare, but to no avail.

"Finch, I know you think I will probably just get in the way tonight, and that you are trying to shield me from any nasty incidents that may occur, and for that I am grateful. But I can't just sit here on my paws whilst you chaps take all the risks. My decision is final."

"Very well, sir. Let's get this operation under way."

And with that, Finch and Henry stepped out into the darkness and loaded a duffel bag and a large portmanteau bag into the boot of the Rolls-Royce before heading off through the busy streets of London, up towards Hampstead.

Chapter 14

They arrived at their destination just before eight o'clock. Finch parked the Rolls-Royce two streets down from the caravan park, close to a public telephone box but away from the nearest street lamp. As they walked back up the street with the two bags, four ominous-looking characters emerged from the shadows and gave Henry quite a fright. Finch introduced him to the Turner twins, Bouncer, and Linton. They all gave a him a firm but respectful handshake. None of them would normally have had much time for a posh cat from Belgravia (especially one who was now in an outfit that looked like he was off to a fancy dress party), but the fact that he had saved Finch's life meant that he had gone up several notches in their estimation.

It was agreed that Bouncer would stay with the Rolls. He kept the ignition on, the V8 engine barely audible as it idled in the night air. Finch instructed him to keep an eye on the phone box as they had given Daphne the number in case of an emergency. Meanwhile, Rick and Mick did a final reconnaissance around the whole caravan park. Everything was quiet, so they gave the signal to the other three to proceed. As they slowly approached the target vehicle, an eerie silence prevailed. A gentle breeze rustled some nearby trees, and the yellow sodium-vapour street lamps cast a light that coloured everything in shades of pale orange and black.

Linton pulled out a small leather pouch from his jacket and extracted some metal instruments. Within ten seconds he had successfully picked the lock on the caravan door and then slowly pulled down the handle, which squeaked very loudly. Or so it seemed to Henry, who jumped two feet in the air but then, being a cat, landed silently back on the ground. The three then proceeded into the caravan. Henry saw the light switch and went to switch it on, but Finch laid a paw on his shoulder and motioned him to stop. It took a minute or two but soon their eyes became accustomed to the low light. The interior of the caravan was dirty and very messy. Since the caravan was quite small, Finch had figured that it should not be too hard to find the painting if it was there, but he hadn't planned for the vast piles of clothes and books and other paraphernalia.

For the next five minutes they had no luck. Searching was a painstaking process as they were extremely careful not to disturb things too much, so as to avoid the obvious signs of a break-in. This involved lifting each item carefully, and only once they had a clear mental image of its location, so that it could be replaced in the exact same position.

Linton approached the kitchen unit that housed the taps and a small sink and was piled high with dirty cups and saucers, cans of condensed milk, and old pizza boxes. Just then, a scary hissing noise came from behind the nearby leather chair. The mongoose froze and signalled to the others to back off towards the door. Then, barely visible in the dim light, a snake emerged from behind the chair. Henry watched as Linton circled the snake, which was motionless, save for its raised head. An epic struggle followed as both animals moved at terrifying speed to attack and counter-attack. Finally the mongoose made a decisive strike, lunging at the snake's head with his sharp fangs. Then it was all over and the snake was dead. The other two animals let out a heavy sigh of relief, but there was no time for high fives or backslapping. The search continued in earnest.

Chapter 15

Meanwhile, at Wiltons, Daphne glanced at the clock. It was just after 8pm. She had rehearsed various subjects of conversation intended to keep Crispin interested and occupied. Finch had told her that ideally she needed to keep him there for at least an hour. Given that it would take him thirty minutes to get back to Hampstead from the restaurant, that should allow them a good hour-and-a-half to go over the caravan.

Benson, the head waiter, had recognised Daphne the moment she had entered the restaurant some fifteen minutes earlier. She wasn't the type of cat you forgot in a hurry, especially if your job was to look after the rich and glamorous. The silver fox seated her at one of the best tables, acceding to her request for a good view of the restaurant's clock. Her chair also faced the front of the restaurant, so she was able to see Crispin straight away when he crashed through the door a few minutes later. As usual, he wore a loud and rather tasteless ensemble that comprised a black-and-white checked tailcoat and bright yellow corduroy trousers with grey alligator-skin boots. He swept brusquely past a small meerkat whose job it was to meet and greet the guests, announcing in a very loud voice to no one in particular (though the whole restaurant heard him) that he had a table booked and wished to be seated immediately.

"Yes, it's with Daphne…" he continued, pausing only when he realised that he did not actually know her surname. "Ah, good evening, my dear," he said as he spotted her at the table, reaching out to kiss her on the cheek, but having to make do with her outstretched paw.

"Crispin, thank you so much for coming. This is long overdue!"

Crispin merely grunted as he swiftly perused the menu. "I'll have a selection of grilled fish and something to drink. You are paying, aren't you, Daphne? You did say it was your treat."

"Indeed," she replied.

"Splendid. Then I'll have a bottle of Dom Pérignon 1973!" he screeched charmlessly as he passed the wine list back to Benson without looking at him.

The fox turned to Daphne with a look that was intended to both confirm the order and express deep contempt for her awful dinner companion. She nodded on both counts.

"So how is Yews Hall, then? Enjoying the generous bequest from my brother, are you?" Crispin inquired with a sneer.

Daphne tried to remain calm, simply responding that all was well and that she looked forward to inviting Crispin down to Sussex soon. She had not seen him since the reading of the will and had forgotten just how unpleasant he was. He was a very awkward character, arrogant and suspicious at the same time. She felt scared and uncomfortable despite all her preparations, which was unusual for her. It was almost as though he had some strange hold over her. She shivered slightly as she searched for something to say.

"Actually, Crispin, whilst I remember, are you still OK to umpire the cricket match next summer? You were sorely missed this year and the villagers were quite upset." A nervous smile played on her lips but she hoped that Crispin was too busy quaffing the champagne to notice.

"Don't you worry, the umpire will strike back; back indeed, in ways that will take your breath away!" He chortled and turned to look at the clock. "So anyway," he asked as he turned back, "what do you want from me? You look nervous, dear." He leered suspiciously at his dinner companion.

"Well, let's wait till we have had some food, shall we? I am starving! It's something you will find very interesting, so we should take our time."

He stared at her for some moments and then merely grunted. Luckily, the awkward pause was interrupted by the arrival of the first course. Daphne took the opportunity to glance surreptitiously at the clock: it was nearly 8.25. As Crispin was tucking into his food voraciously and slurping his champagne, she decided to pop to the toilet quickly to compose herself.

In hindsight, of course, she realised that that was a big mistake. For, as she returned to the restaurant and made her way back to the table, there was no sign of Crispin. She checked with Benson, who confirmed that the cat had dashed out of the restaurant immediately after she had headed downstairs. So she asked for a telephone and made the prearranged emergency call.

Chapter 16

Back at the caravan, they heard a coded knock on the door – two taps, a pause and then three more taps – that told them that one of the Rottweilers was outside. Silently, Finch opened the door to Mick, who reported the news.

"Daphne rang the phone box about three minutes ago and spoke to Bouncer. She thinks Crispin smelled a rat because he slipped out of the restaurant after the first course at around 8.25 whilst she was in the toilet. She rang as soon as she could. So I reckon if he grabs a taxi he could be here by five to nine. We need to be free and clear of the target vehicle a couple of minutes before that to be on the safe side."

"We've got fifteen minutes," whispered Finch. He turned back into the caravan and repeated the same words to Henry and Linton.

Henry had not been idle and, under a dusty kilim rug folded over double, had discovered an old metal safe with a combination lock. It looked like it was at least fifty years old. At an educated guess, it was possibly just about large enough to hold the painting. Although new to this type of caper, he was learning fast. So, rather than jump up and down and shout his success for all to hear, he merely pointed silently to the safe as he turned to Linton and then Finch. The mongoose gave him a nod and moved swiftly over to the safe. Before he did anything he inspected the sides and the door to check for any anti-tampering devices. He then proceeded to put one ear to the lock and move the dial very, very slowly. He didn't need to ask for silence. Henry didn't move a muscle. Indeed, he was barely breathing. After a short time, Linton turned to the others with a huge grin and then gently pulled the handle of the safe door, which swung open silently on well-oiled hinges that belied its age.

There, propped up on its side, was a familiar sight: the painting entitled *The Dogana from the Steps of the Hotel Europa* by J. M. W. Turner. The original picture; not a fake.

Whilst Linton had been busy cracking the safe, Finch had removed the fake painting from its bag. He handed it to the mongoose, who very carefully studied the exact position of the original painting in the safe before replacing it with the fake. He then closed the safe door. Finch instructed the other two to leave the caravan, and pointed to Linton to take the dead snake with them. Although the fact that it was missing might arouse some suspicion, it was less of a telltale sign of a break-in than a dead animal would be. The bulldog took one final look around the caravan before departing silently with the other two. The Turner twins followed, and they all turned into the street where the Rolls-Royce was parked. Henry got into the car as Finch deposited the bag in the boot. The others vanished into the night. The celebrations could wait for now. Indeed, the only other words that the cat uttered that night were "Thank you, Finch", to which the bulldog simply nodded.

As they prepared to head home to Belgravia, in the rear-view mirror of the Rolls-Royce, Finch saw a black taxi driving down the street behind them towards the caravan park. A long cat in a very loud black-and-white jacket was visible in the back. Finch checked the clock in the car. It was 20.54.

Crispin jumped out of the taxi and raced towards the caravan, only remembering to pay the cabbie when he shouted out twice for his fare. He then bounded in, not even stopping to turn on the light. The place was a mess, but it looked like his mess and not one that someone else had made. He flung himself at the safe, and in his haste dialled the wrong combination multiple times before he finally managed to get it open. On seeing an oil painting still inside, he let out a loud and rather wheezy meow of pleasure before collapsing on the floor with a sinister leer on his face. He had failed to notice the absence of the hissing noise which was often to be heard in the caravan.

Chapter 17

Daphne had spent the night at the Cadogan Hotel as planned and as agreed she telephoned Henry's flat early the following morning. Henry was still in bed, but Finch was preparing breakfast. Finding them back safe and sound, Daphne raced round to 77 Eaton Square. Henry, wearing his blue silk polka-dot dressing gown, emerged rubbing his face (which still showed traces of boot polish) as Daphne bounded down the corridor.

"Well?" she gasped.

"Operation Cheesecake was a success," he explained with a grin, before launching into a more detailed summary of the previous night's activity as Finch set the table. Henry concluded his tale with their safe arrival back at Eaton Square. "But what on earth happened at dinner?" he asked. "It was a good job Finch made a plan for an emergency phone call."

"Well, it was all terribly awkward. Crispin was only there out of pure greed, I think, and he soon became very restless. I went to powder my nose, and when I came back he had vanished. So I asked Benson if I could make a phone call and then I spoke to someone and gave the code name as you suggested. Who was that, by the way? He sounded like an enormous dog."

"He is indeed, but very gentle, Finch tells me."

"Well anyway, it looks like it just worked out in the nick of time. Thank you so much, Finch, for looking after Henry like this, and for getting the painting back. And thank all your friends for me too."

"A pleasure, ma'am. It's a pity you didn't see Mr Oxshott's outfit last night. It was quite special. Very black."

"Thank you, Finch," Henry sighed.

"Was it from Harrods?" asked Daphne with a giggle.

"No, actually, it was from… well, never mind" replied Henry, tugging his whiskers.

Finch grinned as he announced that breakfast was served. Henry was in the best of spirits, but as always the bulldog cautioned against any of them lowering their guard. He was sure that Crispin would try again for revenge, and Yews Hall was very likely to be his next target. But for now, at least, they sensed that there was to be a lull in proceedings.

In the back of his mind Henry wondered about the favour that he now owed Daphne in return for her having lured Crispin to Wiltons. As usual, his good breeding prevented him from raising the matter. He was also reassured by the knowledge that she was a rather confident young cat who was not shy in coming forward and asking for what she wanted.

Chapter 18

A few days later, a rather pompous and overdressed young pig was sent by a large auction house based on Bond Street to value a painting. It was suggested by the owner that the painting in question was by J. M. W. Turner and depicted a scene in Venice. Although the caller sounded knowledgeable, the senior director of the auction house was very sceptical when he discovered that the address to be visited was a small caravan, so he decided to send his most junior member of staff on what he was now convinced was a fool's errand.

Crispin was somewhat disappointed to open the door to the pig in question; barely out of art school and yet ready to begin his auction career in earnest.

"Mr Oxshott?"

"Yes, that's me," lied Crispin.

"I am Sebastian Wynstanley from the auction house." The pig looked at the caravan with some disdain, not terribly keen to enter. "I understand you have a painting that you believe to be by Turner."

"Oh, it's a Turner all right, don't you worry, laddie!" said

Crispin, rubbing his paws in expectation. "Come in and I'll get it out of the safe."

Wynstanley wiped his feet. He wasn't sure why he had bothered as the soles of his shoes were cleaner than the caravan floor, but it was too late now as he entered the dark and smelly caravan. Crispin fussed over the combination to the safe and then eventually opened the door. Carefully, he took out the picture and propped it up on the desk. The pig asked if they could draw the curtains as that would afford a little more light for the examination, and the cat reluctantly obliged, grumbling as he did so.

Sebastian peered closely at the painting, gulped slightly and then turned slowly to Crispin, struggling for words. "Well, sir, I am sure this painting means a lot to you…"

"It certainly does," replied Crispin with something between a snigger and a cackle.

"And it must be of enormous sentimental value?" continued the pig with some trepidation.

"It certainly is, knowing that it's mine now, and no longer in the hands of that nincompoop."

"Quite," said the pig, who was now feeling very wary of this cat.

"So how much is it worth, then? Two million? Three?" rasped Crispin greedily.

"Well," replied Sebastian, "as I said, given its sentimental value to you, it's priceless, really."

"Priceless, you say?" said Crispin, not really understanding what he meant.

"All I mean is that it's priceless to *you*, and that's all that matters, isn't it?" Sebastian Wynstanley was playing for time.

Crispin just stared at him menacingly with his one good eye, waiting for him to continue.

"So it's really not important that it's only a worthless copy, and a rather poor one at that!" the pig added, laughing rather nervously. No one had told him that this job would involve visiting rusty old caravans to look at terrible copies of works by famous artists. He'd thought he would be spending all his time in beautiful stately homes discovering original masterpieces by Rembrandt or Picasso.

Crispin stared at the pig as he tried to make sense of what he was being told.

Wynstanley noticed a small card on the back of the painting and picked it up. He thought it might ease the tension if he read it out what was written on it. "'Dear Crispin, over the last year I have come to love the original of this picture. I hope you enjoy this cheap copy of it too.' Oh, isn't that nice?" The pig smiled weakly before he made a swift exit.

And at that point all that could be heard from the caravan was an ear-splitting screech from a one-eyed cat who realised he had been well and truly done over.

Matador

For exclusive discounts on Matador titles,
sign up to our occasional newsletter at
troubador.co.uk/bookshop